# It was pinch-me-and-I-might-wake-up unbelievable.

Standing here looking at the sandstone and clapboard structure, her heart pitter-pattered with delight, and once again she felt a little like Cinderella at the ball. It was as if she had the entire summer before the carriage turned back into a pumpkin. All she had to do was stand up for her rights....

"No," she said more firmly this time as a slow burn of excitement and determination kindled inside of her. "Look. I moved in here with the assurance that you were okay with this. Wyatt said if you had a problem with it, he would take care of it. And besides that, I signed a lease. *And* I've already sublet my apartment for the summer."

Seth's expression darkened, and Melody looked down and thought once more about running. But she wasn't going anywhere. She was staying—unless he threw her over his broad shoulder and carried her off.

## Books by Debra Clopton

Love Inspired

*The Trouble with
  Lacy Brown
*And Baby Makes Five
*No Place Like Home
*Dream a Little Dream
*Meeting Her Match
*Operation: Married
  by Christmas
*Next Door Daddy

*Mule Hollow

*Her Baby Dreams
*The Cowboy Takes a Bride
*Texas Ranger Dad
*Small-Town Brides
  "A Mule Hollow Match"
*Lone Star Cinderella

## DEBRA CLOPTON

was a 2004 Golden Heart finalist in the inspirational category, a 2006 Inspirational Readers' Choice Award winner, a 2007 Golden Quill award winner and a finalist for the 2007 American Christian Fiction Writers Book of the Year Award. She praises the Lord each time someone votes for one of her books, and takes it as an affirmation that she is exactly where God wants her to be.

Debra is a hopeless romantic and loves to create stories with lively heroines and the strong heroes who fall in love with them. But most importantly she loves showing her characters living their faith, seeking God's will in their lives one day at a time. Her goal is to give her readers an entertaining story that will make them smile, hopefully laugh and always feel God's goodness as they read her books. She has found the perfect home for her stories writing for the Love Inspired line and still has to pinch herself just to see if she really is awake and living her dream.

When she isn't writing she enjoys taking road trips, reading and spending time with her two sons, Chase and Kris. She loves hearing from readers and can be reached through her Web site, www.debraclopton.com, or at P.O. Box 1125, Madisonville, Texas 77864.

# Lone Star Cinderella
## Debra Clopton

Steeple
Hill®

Published by Steeple Hill Books™

STEEPLE HILL BOOKS

Steeple
Hill®

Recycling programs
for this product may
not exist in your area.

ISBN-13: 978-0-373-81415-2

LONE STAR CINDERELLA

www.SteepleHill.com

Printed in U.S.A.

Whether you turn to the right or the left,
your ears will hear a voice behind you saying,
This is the way; walk in it.
—-*Isaiah* 30:21

This book is dedicated to my mom and dad.
I love you so much.

# Chapter One

Something was wrong. Melody Chandler knew it even before the distinctive sound broke the silence of the blistering Texas afternoon. Turning away from the hundred-year-old stagecoach house, she shielded her eyes against the glare of the June sun. The black pickup sped ominously toward her, dust billowing behind it like a villainous cloak—not at all helping the picture of doom her mind had already conjured up.

Her insides went queasy as she watched the truck bound over the dirt road bisecting several pastures before forcing its way into the stage-coach yard. Wyatt Turner, the man who had given her the opportunity to live in this wonderful old relic for the next few months, had pointed out that the path the truck was roaring down was the actual track followed by the stagecoaches in the 1800s. *Amazing!*

To think; she was standing where pioneers had waited, watching their stagecoaches lumber toward them. As a history teacher, she could well imagine how it had looked back then and how excited they must have felt…unfortunately excitement wasn't what she was feeling.

Cotton-mouthed, she clasped her sweaty palms behind her back. She knew it was hopeless the second she met the glare of the cowboy behind the wheel. No doubt about it, Seth Turner had come to tell her to kiss her sweet setup goodbye.

She'd known it was too good to be true. Wasn't that the way it always turned out when something came too easily?

Her stomach jumped when her gaze locked with Seth's stormy eyes through the windshield. Did he even begin to understand the power he wielded with one look from those gorgeous brown eyes?

Oh, yeah, he understood.

But today this wasn't a someone-to-watch-over-you kind of look. His frown crossed the distance and snapped her right out of her fanciful musing to the reality of the moment.

She gave a weak smile and immediately turned his frown into an all-out scowl—which was still gorgeous…and totally ridiculous for her to be noticing. Especially as all six foot two of him climbed out of the large truck and stalked toward her.

She told her feet to move, to go meet him, not to just stand there like a rabbit caught in a trap. But that was a hard thing to do when her feet only wanted to move in the opposite direction! She settled for being satisfied to just hold her ground with quaking knees.

"Hello, Seth," she said with a wobble, extending her hand. "Melody. Melody Chandler."

Looking slightly confused, he gave her hand a momentary pump. "I, uh, know who you are."

Her cheeks warmed. "Sorry." Of course he knew who she was. Mule Hollow was so small that even if they'd never actually had a conversation, he had to know her name. "It's the teacher in me." Not the greatest comeback but at least it was something.

He shifted his weight from one boot to the other. "Look, I'm not sure what Wyatt was thinking. But, I'm afraid my brother didn't have the authority to rent this place out to you."

It was the boot all right, just as she'd thought. Her heart sank. Wyatt shared ownership of the ranch and the stagecoach house with his brother

Seth and their other brother Cole. But everyone knew Seth was the brother in charge of the ranch. He lived here, after all, and had been out of town.

"But," she blurted. "He did, though. To me." *As if the man didn't already know this!*

"Yes. But he shouldn't have. He knew I didn't want the place occupied."

Every great comeback known to man raced through Melody's mind—and kept right on going. "Oh," was all that came out. It was always that way with her. *Always.*

"So you're okay with that?"

Was he really asking her that? The word *no* came to mind but not to her mouth—her mouth remained shut as if she'd mistakenly used a glue stick instead of ChapStick.

*No*, she wasn't good with that, but she had to say something. Make her case. Instead, feeling the spirit of the wonderful place slipping away from her, she turned to stare at the rugged old house. She'd felt like Cinderella with this opportunity, but Cinderella lasted at least a third of the way through the ball and here she was being run off already.

How could he even ask if she was okay with this? Of course she didn't want to leave. Sure she could do her research somewhere else, and had originally planned to do exactly that. But this had been the golden opportunity. Immersing herself in the atmosphere of the past had given her a thrill of excitement that she'd never experienced before. And now, with barely a how-do-you-do, Seth was sending her packing.

"Look," he said, not unkindly. "I'll help you move your things back to town. I'm sure you'll be able to get your apartment back before Adela rents it out."

She just blinked, too stunned to move. She didn't want her apartment back.

*Then say so—just say no.*

Why was it she had learned to exert her authority over her classroom—well, most of the time anyway—yet, when it came to men she just *thought* about what she wanted to say? It was infuriating. Her brother's face slid into her imagination and something rebelled. "No." It was barely audible, but she'd said it.

"*Excuse* me?"

It was one thing to talk big in the mirror. It was a completely other thing to actually stand up for herself. Looking at Seth she just knew she had to tell him no. This was one of the most important moments in her life. She needed to be here, in this house. She *was* spending her summer researching stagecoach robbers and hidden treasure! It was unbelievable.

To Melody, it was pinch-me-and-I-might-wake up unbelievable. Some would think her "quest" was a frivolous waste of time and simply a weak diversionary tactic. Which was true, in part—she'd do anything to find a way *not* to think about her brother.

But the truth was, she was ready for frivolous.

Past ready! She *needed* frivolous…more than anyone could possibly know or understand. Wyatt had dropped this opportunity into her lap, and she just couldn't give it up. Something told her this was her one chance to make a difference in her life. That it was now or never.

But needing something and going out and getting it were two different things. No. This—this wonderful opportunity—had actually just happened. It was a God thing.

When all the pieces fell into place like they had, there was no way it could be anything but a God thing. When she'd decided to do the research, it had been her small effort at an escape from the pressures she was feeling about her brother and his problems. But the fact that her research led her to this 1800s stagecoach house, the fact that it was not more than ten miles from where she was living, the fact that Wyatt had *offered* her the opportunity to live inside this wonderful place for the summer…that was God. It was remarkable.

More so because she was Melody Chandler, aka unremarkable fourth grade history teacher, background prop for all occasions, pushover.

Sadly they were all accurate descriptions of her. And exactly what she knew a man like Seth would be thinking about her…

But standing here looking at the sandstone-and-clapboard structure, her heart pitter-pattered once more with delight, and once again she felt a little like Cinderella at the ball. It was as if she had the entire summer before the carriage turned back into a pumpkin. All she had to do was stand up for her rights…

"No," she said more firmly this time as a slow burn of excitement and determination kindled inside of her. "Look. I moved in here with the assurance that you were okay with this. Wyatt said if you had a problem with it, he would take care of it. And besides that, I signed a lease. *And* I've already sublet my apartment for the summer."

Seth's expression turned into a mixture of confusion and disbelief. "You have a lease?" He clearly couldn't believe his ears. The man looked as immovable as the nearly two-hundred-year-old rock fireplace running up the side of the stage-coach house.

She took a lesson from his attitude and stood her ground. She ran her damp palms down the side of her jeans. "I'm *not* leaving." *Not* came out as a squeak but was obviously decipherable since Seth's brows dipped beneath the brim of his Stetson. Her nerve faltered. "I'm not harming anything."

Had she really said that?

Seth's eyes narrowed and his lean jaw twitched. "Seriously. I want you to leave," he said, as if she'd just made a joke. "The last thing I want is someone out here researching Sam Bass and hidden treasure and all of that nonsense."

*Nonsense!* How dare he think her work was nonsense. How dare he think he could just decide he wanted her out and she would scamper off. "Seriously. I'm staying," she said and almost passed out at the effort behind her words.

His look of disbelief was almost comical. And there was a good reason—she imagined his surprise had something to do with the fact that she'd been a wallflower for the past two years! He hadn't expected to see her ever speaking!

The corners of his eyes twitched slightly as their gazes held fast. She was holding her breath, bluffing her way through this.

His gaze dropped, slid over her, taking in her ratty jeans, her dusty T-shirt and her flip-flops as if sizing her up as an opponent. Sadly, he would find her lacking in more ways than she wanted to think about. A bit shaken by his frank stare, she clung to her newfound nerve and forced herself to step toward him.

"You have a treasure trove of information inside this wonderful building. History that is just languishing away in there. Don't you want to know what it is?"

He crossed his arms over his chest. "Frankly, no."

As a true lover of history, someone who enjoyed learning everything about the past and also passing that knowledge on to others, she couldn't understand his attitude.

"But you have journals in there that might tell us who was on the land. Why who knows, a president or, or even Sam Bass himself might have stood right where you're standing a hundred and fifty years ago. Aren't you curious?"

"No."

"But it's *history*. Just think of the possibilities. I mean when I found out this fantastic place was sitting out here I got goose bumps. To think, right here not ten miles from my apartment is this amazing historic wonderland—I'm getting them all over again just talking about it." On impulse she held out her arm. "See. Right there."

He glanced at her arm like she was a crazy woman. She was babbling again, but it was because of her love affair with history. She'd always studied history from a bookworm point of view. But this—oh, this was different. Maybe explaining it would change his mind.

"When I called here, thinking I would be talking to you, I just wanted to look at the place, because of the research I was doing. I never dreamed you and your family had all of these original journals stored inside the house—it is mind-boggling.

"Your brother showed them to me. He was an unbelievably nice man, so accommodating. It was Wyatt's suggestion that I move out here and mix research for your family in with my own—he said there were some blank spots in the journals that my research might be able to fill in. You just can't *not* want this done."

His expression darkened—if that were even possible. "I not only can't but *don't* want it done. What I do want is for you to agree to back out of that lease agreement. Knowing Wyatt acted without my consent should make you want to do the right thing."

The man was infuriating.

Who wouldn't want this? *Who?* "You don't get it," she said, totally amazed at herself. "The research I'm doing could very well alter or add new data to the history books. Sam Bass is Texas's most-documented stagecoach- and train-robber, but it is the legends that have grown over the years that intrigue me. To think that he is rumored to have buried treasure all over Texas that was never recovered. There is a very real possibility that he may have robbed the stage on its way to this stop and then hid the treasure on your property. Don't you want me to see if that's true?"

"That's exactly the reason I don't want you here. You're going to bring all that hidden-treasure nonsense to everyone's attention and the next thing I know the place will be overrun with treasure-hunting nuts."

Melody bristled. "I can't believe you just said *that.* I mean, really—you own a piece of the great American West! A piece of Texas history and folklore. My goodness, you have a true treasure in this place. Forget the buried stuff." She waved her hand at the stagecoach house. "No telling what history is here and all you can think about is keeping a few men with metal detectors and shovels off your property!"

She couldn't believe she'd said that and with such force. By the look on his face, Seth couldn't either.

It felt insanely satisfying.

"Are you finished?"

Was she? She could almost see him gearing up to tell her once more she had to leave. It made her want to pull her hair out in more ways than one. "Yes," she said, deflating. Had the last five minutes all been a charade?

"*No*," she added. "I need to say this…I—I'm going to stay. I have a legal right."

Seth's expression darkened, and Melody looked down and thought once more about running. But she wasn't going anywhere. She was staying— unless he threw her over his broad shoulder and hauled her off…and he could do that as easily as she could carry off a stuffed toy. "I did sign the lease." She suddenly remembered how Wyatt had grinned when he presented her with the lease. He'd known this was how his brother was going to react to her being here! He'd leveraged her position on purpose—the plot thickened…Wyatt wanted her here just as much as she wanted to be here. But why? "Look. While I know you might not want me here, I *promise* you're not going to regret it."

His lips flattened, and he had the oddest look in

his eyes. A huge lump lodged in her windpipe and her resolve started to crumble—but he suddenly spun on his heels, stalked to his truck and disappeared in a cloud of dust. Just like he'd arrived.

Only then did it dawn on her..."I'm still here," she said, turning slowly to look at the house. And as she took a step toward it, she smiled all the way to her toes.

## Chapter Two

She'd stood her ground! A delicious sense of pride and disbelief curled its way through Melody.

And with *Seth Turner* of all people.

Seth was outgoing, totally dashing and self-assured—that is, when he wasn't upset as he had been just now. Obviously, not getting his own way didn't suit him. They were polar opposites in every way. No one recognized that more than she did. She hovered in the background, forgettable in her quietness, while Seth was unforgettable. When the man entered a room, you noticed. When the man *left* a room, you noticed. Consequently, women flocked around him.

She should know, she'd watched from afar—as in far across the room—for two years. And she'd gotten the idea watching him that he took his female adoration for granted. As if he didn't care one way or the other that the women were there, he just expected they would be. Oddly that just seemed to draw them all the more. Women were weird like that sometimes.

Understanding her limitations and shortcomings she'd admired him from a distance. So much so that she almost hadn't called to ask if she could see the stagecoach house in the first place.

Who would have thought all of that would lead to her watching him speed off into the hot summer heat, temper blazing? Without a doubt, she would never have had this opportunity if he'd been the one to pick up the phone that day.

She wasn't exactly sure what the two brothers had going on between them but thank goodness she'd signed a lease.

Why was Seth so against the idea of her being here?

That put a damper on the pride she felt for having stood up for her rights. But really, when she'd decided to do this research on outlaw Sam Bass it had been because she desperately needed a distraction from her life. Lately she'd begun to feel a complete and utter lack of respect for herself. And it felt wrong to feel so much resentment toward her brother…and even her parents to some extent, God rest their souls. But lately, as her brother, Ty, had continued his roller-coaster ride of alcohol and drugs, expecting that she would always be there to pay his way like her parents had, she'd begun to feel trapped. Guilt riddled her and turmoil had begun to rule her life once more. Just as it did every time Ty went off the wagon and started using again. No matter what she did with her life, she'd realized that Ty ruled it. And she didn't know what to do.

The idea of losing herself in researching Sam Bass and the hidden treasure had come to her late one night when she was reading and trying to forget a particularly nasty phone exchange she'd had with Ty…she had to admit that sometimes she wanted to run away. It was hard dealing with Ty and everything—treasure hunting seemed like such a fascinating escape.

It had been the depth of her stress level that had given her the courage to make the call to tour the stagecoach house. And it had been the thought of losing this great opportunity that had caused her to stand her ground against Seth Turner.

And now, she had a new mystery that intrigued her. Hurrying inside the stagecoach house, she wondered what was in those journals that would make Seth want to keep them secret.

The only way to find out was to read them.

She headed straight to the hall closet where they were stored in an 1800s strongbox. Grabbing hold of the brass handles, she dragged the heavy wooden chest out into the open and lifted the lid. When Wyatt had shown the journals to her she'd been curious, but she was so excited about her own research that she hadn't yet looked inside of them. Now Seth's reaction had her full attention, and she was compelled to find out what it was he was so concerned about.

"Let's see what you're hiding," she mumbled. Picking up the first journal, she sat cross-legged on the floor and began to read.

Seth *already* regretted it as he stormed into his house. Yanking open the fridge door and pulling out a soda, he popped the tab so hard the metal ring flew across the room and bounced off his John Deere calendar. What had his foolhardy brother been thinking?

Seth took a long drink of the dark liquid feeling the flavor burn its way down his throat. Restless, he crushed the can in his hand before stalking to his office. He slouched into his chair as he grabbed the phone and jabbed his brother's number into the keypad. He waited for what seemed like an eternity but was really only four rings before Wyatt picked up.

"You better be glad there's three hundred miles between us right now—"

"Man, I knew it!"

"Knew what?"

"Knew that timid woman would get to you. Got to me. I couldn't help myself."

"You couldn't help yourself? What kinda crazy, cockamamy story is that? If you couldn't help yourself, then fine, give her the tour and be done with it. But *don't* have her sign a lease and move her in on my turf."

Wyatt bellowed with laughter.

"Stop laughing. This isn't funny. You know good and well I don't want her out there rifling through Grandma Jane's journals." Grandma Jane was actually his great-great-great-great-great-grandmother, but growing up knowing their family tree like they did had its problems when telling stories. Seth and his brothers had shortened all their grandparents to Grandpa or Grandma and followed it with their first name. It made life easier.

Wyatt groaned over the line. "Seth, man. You and I both know she's not going to find anything in them. We've both read them, and there is no truth in the tall tales Gramps spouted off all those years ago. Would you just relax? Look, I have to go or I'll be late."

"Hey," Seth snapped but the line was already dead. More disgruntled than ever, Seth leaned back in his chair and stared at his black computer screen. He envisioned Melody Chandler's bright eyes staring out at him. Wyatt would have been as surprised as he was to see nothing timid in those eyes today. Where had the woman he'd met today come from? The plain Jane he'd seen around town for the last couple of years seemed reserved and…well, to be brutally honest, boring.

The woman he'd encountered today had eyes that caught the light with her enthusiasm and indignation. Today those eyes sparkled like his mother's amethyst brooch. It had been amazing. How had he never noticed them before?

*Because you never looked before.*

True. He tried to think if he'd ever actually been close enough to have seen the richness of color in them…he came up empty. Matter of fact, he'd bet the closest he'd ever come to her was when he'd attended the singles Sunday school class—not that he went to Sunday school class often. He was more of a congregation man. And he was certain that when he was in the auditorium that Melody

Chandler was always clear across the room from him. He had noticed her over there, though. Noticed that she was one of those women who seemed to sit down and grow smaller. Like she drew into herself. She looked neither to the left or the right as she listened to the preacher's words. Personally, he thought she looked like she'd locked herself up in a box.

But today she'd seemed stronger. Bolder. He smiled thinking of how she'd puffed up and glared at him. Of course he could tell she was bluffing…one thing about his great-great-great-great-great-Grandpa Oakley—just plain Grandpa Oakley for short—was that he'd known a bluff from a mile away. It was said that when it came to poker the man hadn't needed to lie or cheat. That he won at poker because he could read people…it was a trait he'd passed down to Seth. And he'd thought he was pretty good at it until today.

No doubt about it; Melody would have grabbed her bags and hit the road back to town the split second he'd snapped "git."

All he had to do was push a tad harder and she'd vacate his property—rental contract or not. And that was the kicker—why hadn't he pressed and sent her running?

Because he was intrigued and surprised…and that hadn't happened to him in a very long time.

"I still ain't believin' that them three gals went on a cruise," Applegate Thornton was saying the next morning when Seth walked into Sam's Diner. "If that ship knows what's good fer it it'll ban Norma Sue and Esther Mae from the sun deck."

"And what about yor fair-skinned Adela, Sam? She could come home fried like a lobster," Stanley said.

Seth took his seat at the counter beside another cowboy, Luke Burns. He was sipping his coffee and listening to the conversation like the entertainment that it was. App and Stanley were longtime buddies and spent most mornings at the front window table in battle over their checkerboard. Like most of the men around town Seth liked getting to the diner before they left so he could hear what the two men had to say.

"Y'all don't need ta be a worry'n about my wife. Adela's got more sense in her pinky than you two got combined. She'll be wearin' a hat and plenty of sunscreen." The wiry little man plunked a white coffee cup in front of Seth and filled it in one fluid movement.

"Now don't go getting all riled up, Sam," Applegate practically hollered—not because he was mad, just half deaf and too stubborn to keep his hearing aid on. "All's I'm sayin' is them three could git into trouble off out thar in the Atlantic. I ain't believin' you, Roy Don and Hank let um go."

Sam scowled at his old friend. "Let um go? Them's three grown women with independent minds. They got this idea 'cause us fellas didn't want ta set foot on that floating Titanic so they went without us."

Applegate, thin as a toothpick and as dour as a pickle, looked from Stanley to Sam. "You scared of the water?"

Sam nodded. "Yup, and I'm man enough to admit it."

Luke chuckled and drew a glare from Sam. "Son, I might be short and twice yor age but I kin kick yor sorry hide right out of that thar door."

"No offense, Sam, but you got to admit it's sorta funny."

Sam snorted and crossed his arms as he glared at all of them. It was clear that he was in no mood to be messed with. To their surprise, he suddenly threw his hands up in the air. "Y'all ignore my ill temper. I'm missing my Adela somethin' fierce. We ain't been apart since we got married a year ago."

Seth grinned. "That explains it then." Sam and Adela were newlyweds. And the diner owner was head over heels in love with his longtime love.

"When are they coming home?" Seth asked.

"Six days, five hours and thirty-two minutes."

Luke shook his head and laid his money on the table. "That's just sad, Sam. It's just wrong to be that tied down."

Seth half expected Sam to fly around the counter and take Luke down before he got out of the diner but instead he wagged his head. "Poor cowpoke. He don't have a clue what he's sayin'."

"Yup," Applegate barked. "Thar ain't nothin' like the love of a good woman. Ain't that right, Stanley?"

"Yep. Right." Stanley never lifted his gaze from the checkerboard. He rubbed his plump chin then grinned as he reached for his checker and made his move. "Gotcha!"

"Oh, phoo," Applegate snapped. Standing, he snatched up his Stetson and settled it precisely on his head. "Come on, ya old coot. We got ta get to play practice."

Stanley beamed like a flare as he raked the checkers into a pouch then folded the board. "I've done whupped ya every game this week, App. You gonna concede that I'm the better player?"

App snatched up the half-full five-pound bag of

sunflower seeds and marched toward the door without saying a word.

Stanley, on the other hand, looked like a rooster with his chest thrown out so far it was a wonder he didn't throw out his hip. "See y'all," he drawled and caught the swinging door as App disappeared through it. "Come on, App," he called. "Ya gotta admit it some day. I'm the better player."

App's snort could be heard even though the door had swung shut behind them. They also helped out with the lights at the barn theater on the outskirts of town. With the Fourth of July just around the bend, Seth knew the theater was planning a special production.

"Those two are something," he said, turning back to Sam.

"Somethin' else. They need themselves some new wives. Bein' widowers all these years ain't good fer the old snoops."

Seth wrapped his hands around the warm coffee cup as Sam topped it off. "Maybe Adela and her cohorts can put their talent to work and hook them up when they get home from this cruise."

Norma Sue, Esther Mae and Adela loved matchmaking and had even placed an ad a couple of years back that brought single women to Mule

Hollow to marry the lonesome local cowboy population. The town had been on the brink of dying back then, but their efforts had totally revitalized the community of three hundred—give or take a handful.

Sam cocked his head to the side and studied Seth. "I'm 'fraid thar might not be any hope fer them two. But you better be on the lookout when them girls get home."

Seth grunted and took a swig of coffee, deciding he wasn't touching that comment with a ten foot pole.

"So how thangs goin' with that sweet Melody livin' in the stagecoach house?"

"Fine, I guess." He'd been so focused on his own reasons for not wanting her digging into his family history that he hadn't thought about what others would be saying.

"What does that mean?"

"I just saw her briefly yesterday when I got back into town. *Right* after I read my brother's note filling me in on his little joke. Y'all knew she was moving in out there before I did."

Sam hooted with laughter. "Me and the boys kinda wondered if ole Wyatt was pulling a fast one on ya." Bob Denton and Will Sutton came through the door and took a booth. Seth gave them a nod as Sam grabbed the coffeepot. "I'll be right back. Don't run off."

Seth nursed his coffee, surprised Sam and his buddies hadn't started teasing him the minute he walked into the diner. He wasn't exactly in the mood for it. Melody Chandler had the ability to change his life with that research she was doing. It wasn't a teasing matter…

He kept thinking about how her face lit up when she talked about searching through all the historical documents. He figured it was only natural for history teachers to get excited about history, but this was a bit over the top. It nagged at him all night.

For nearly two years, she'd blended into the background of Mule Hollow gatherings with her quiet personality. He simply couldn't get over how a light had seemed to flash on inside of her when she was talking about her research.

"So, like I was saying, how's that goin'?" Sam said, rounding the counter and settling the pot back on the burner. "I practically forgot that old camp house was a stagecoach stop at one time. It's been a long time since anyone said anything about it."

"Yeah, and that's just how I wanted it to be. A camp house," Seth grunted. "I don't know how Melody found out about it being out there." His mood swung low, and he didn't try to hide it.

Sam grinned. "Research. Or so my Adela tells me. She started askin' a few questions and there ya have it, the perfect opportunity fer Wyatt to waylay ya with his surprise. I remember when the three of you boys were growin' up, y'all always pulled tricks on each other. And little Cole usually got the worst end of it."

"True, but this is different. I don't know what Wyatt was thinking."

Sam lifted his bushy brows. "Look on the bright side, that little gal shor is purdy when her eyes light up."

Seth met Sam's laughing eyes. "You noticed that?"

"Been wonderin' when one of you fool cowboys was gonna notice."

"I noticed," Seth grumbled. "But that doesn't change the fact that I really don't want her out there digging through all the documentation—"

"And why exactly is that?"

Seth leaned in close. "You remember last year when Molly wrote that article about Bob and all those crazy women came to town stalking him?" Molly was the local newspaper reporter who had a syndicated column about life in Mule Hollow. It wasn't every town that advertised for wives, and her column was entertaining enough that it had drawn readers from across the nation. When she'd written an article about what a great catch Bob was, all manner of wacko women had converged on the town to try and win his heart.

Sam glanced toward Bob and chuckled. "Who could forget that? It was somethin' else."

"Well, that's what I think will happen again to some degree if Melody was to turn up anything that would hint that some buried stagecoach loot was buried on my property or anywhere else around here. I don't want that to happen."

Sam wiped the spotless counter with a damp rag and looked sideways at him. "I don't know, it might be plum entertainin'."

Seth stood up to leave. "And that's the problem. I'm just not up for being people's entertainment."

"Then maybe you should help Melody out. You know, contain the situation."

The idea settled over Seth. "That's not a bad idea."

"And you can have it for free."

Sam grinned and Seth did the same. "Thanks. See you later."

He walked out of the diner and was immediately confronted by the changes that had happened in his town over the last couple years. Mule Hollow's weathered buildings had been painted. Not a nice gray or a sedate, eye-pleasing tan or brown. Oh, no. The one- and two-story buildings had been painted every color inside a gumball machine. It even had a hot-pink hair salon that stood out against the horizon like a beacon—he glanced across the street and cringed looking at Heavenly Inspirations Hair Salon. Yep, that *still* took some getting used to. His brothers were always telling him he was too settled in his ways…getting old before his time. What did they know?

His town had changed, and he could deal with it because it didn't intrude on his life on his quiet ranch.

But Melody and her research could potentially change everything…

His mind rolled over what he wanted to do as he drove out of town.

Sam's advice made sense. He could stick his head in the ground and hope nothing turned up that would alter life as he knew it. Or he could help and control what turned up.

He glanced into his rearview mirror as Mule Hollow disappeared. There were some things in this world a man couldn't control. And then there were those things he could.

## Chapter Three

The writings of Jane Turner enthralled Melody. The woman's meticulous documentation of the comings and goings of all who had passed through the doors of the stagecoach house during the 1870s was astonishing. Melody wasn't sure how long Jane had continued her documenting—since she was reading as fast as she could but still had several journals to go—but she was having a wonderful time getting to know Jane and her son.

There were holes in the story, though, Melody quickly realized before heading off to bed to finally try and get some sleep. The number one question was what was Jane's husband doing while she and her son ran the stagecoach house? She hardly ever mentioned him—Melody had calculated he would be Seth's great-great-great-great-

great-grandfather—seven generations! Oakley was his name, and she knew this was the man who had won the place in a poker game. So she was all the more curious as to why barely a mention of him made it into Jane's writings.

In the end, Melody had gone to sleep well after midnight with more questions than answers. She woke early to the sound of rain and with a burning desire to plunge back into the journals. The historian inside of her was engaged completely.

Loving the sound of rain, she put on a pot of coffee and then opened the front door and lifted the windows on the front porch. There couldn't be a better mixture to read to than the fresh scent of rain and coffee combined. It was just a lovely, lovely day. There was a sense of anticipation, and she even felt a little bit of intrigue for what she might find out today. Maybe it was just the history teacher in her…as silly as it sounded, she even felt a bit of *Indiana Jones* nostalgia—not that she was about to find anything nearly as exciting as in the movie. Escape in a book adventure was the best she could ever hope for. And something about these journals excited her as much or more than her Sam Bass research.

Taking a deep breath of the damp fresh air, she strode back to the kitchen ready for business. She poured her coffee, stirred in a heavy dose of cream and a heavier dose of sugar, made herself a quick peanut butter sandwich then settled into her chair at the kitchen table. She'd moved all the journals there the night before after her legs cramped from sitting on the pine floors for several hours. She'd just started reading when the ringing of the telephone jolted her from the past and into the present.

*Ty.* Her palms dampened as she stared at the phone. Was it her brother?

Maybe she just wouldn't answer it—it was a horrible thing to think but there it was. She might just be a rotten person, and a rotten person just wouldn't answer the phone.

For the last few days, she'd been inaccessible because the phone lines hadn't been switched. She'd felt an amazing sense of relief realizing that while she had no phone service her brother couldn't reach her. For four days now she hadn't had to worry about him calling, hadn't had to worry about his demands for money. Oh, she'd thought of him, but she hadn't been overwhelmed by him. Her research had helped, too, just like she'd hoped. But now, with the ringing of the phone, she realized how much that particular detail had helped.

Guilt crawled over her like the clinging poison

oak vines that grew on the fence outside, choking her with its tenacity. She lived on a teacher's salary with a very frugal lifestyle, in part because of her brother's continual bouts with drug addiction. His addictions had been a financial drain on her parents, and now on her own life. Not talking to him was the coward's way out. But then, obviously, she was a coward.

When she'd taken the job here in this remote little town, she'd hoped distance from him would help. She'd hoped her moving would somehow change things. But she'd been wrong. She'd not been able to tell him no and had continued to pay his debts. He was her brother. Her only close living relative, and standing up to him or watching him suffer was just a hard thing to do. Especially knowing that when she tried it he blew a gasket and flew off the handle.

*But, you just stood up to Seth Turner, his scowling expression and all…* Yes, she had. The phone continued to ring and she knew without a doubt that it was Ty on the other end. He would let it ring on and on. Maybe she could stand up to Ty this time…he had to stop using. He had to.

The ringing seemed to grow louder and more insistent as she crossed the room. Taking a deep breath, she reached for the phone. Her hand shook.

Thoughts of Ty always did this to her. She reminded herself that she felt like a doormat being used and abused by his life choices. Out of control.

Ty was thirty years old and had been in and out of trouble for most of his life. Reckless, *selfish* and he had an unbelievable sense of entitlement. And that would be why he was calling her, because he couldn't make his rent payments. For her, living with his addictions had become like a revolving door. Her parents had tried repeatedly to help him and had spent money they couldn't afford in their attempt to help him.

How could it be that he was eighteen months older than her, yet he seemed younger? How could two people raised by the same parents be so different?

She bit her lip. How many times had she asked herself these questions? "Enough times." She closed her eyes, stilled her soul for the sound of his voice—she loved her brother but she hated the life he lived…the life that bled into hers and held her captive.

"Hello."

"Where have you been?"

She stilled her heart against his accusatory tone. "I've been moving."

"You move out of that hick town?"

"No," she said. "I'm still here. Just in a different place."

He snorted. "I'm glad *you* have options. My landlord of this dump I'm in is giving me a hard time again 'cause I didn't get your check yet."

He hadn't gotten it because she hadn't sent it. This was his only reason for ever calling her, and he didn't even ask anymore. Just expected that she would send him the money. Her hand hurt from her death grip on the phone, and she gave herself a silent pep talk.

Deep down she knew she couldn't continue to support him and his addiction. But there was the promise—she pushed it out of her head. He'd chosen this irresponsible lifestyle. He was not a child and he didn't want to change. "Ty, I'm not going to send you any money." The words startled her, even knowing they needed to be said. "I asked you to admit yourself into the county rehab when I sent the last check. Remember, I said that if you didn't it would be my last check—"

"Oh, yeah, what am I supposed to do?" he shouted. "*Huh?* Live on the street?"

She closed her eyes praying for answers she knew weren't going to come. God just didn't seem to care about this part of her life. It was upsetting. "You know I love you, Ty. But," she lost her voice as anger and despair warred inside of her. The phone shook as her hand began to tremble. This man was her brother—*the brother who'd used their parents over and over again. Just like he had to her for the last three years!* Just like he would continue to do if she didn't change something. "…but I can't keep doing this—"

"*Odee*, I lost my job, have a heart. It'll just be until I get my feet on the ground."

She hated when he used the nickname. He'd given it to her when they were toddlers and it reminded her of a time when she thought her big brother could do no wrong. A time before adolescence, when choices were easy.

Tears burned her eyes and tightened her throat. "Me sending you money isn't going to help you. You need help, and I don't know what else to do but say no," the last word was a whisper, that tore out of her. "I'm s-sorry—"

"Sorry! You call yourself a Christian—you hypocrite. If you loved me you'd help me," he shouted and spun off into a string of profanity.

"I don't have to listen to this," Melody said, realizing it was the truth. Angered and humiliated, she slammed the phone down as the tears started. She felt so helpless, and she hated it. And she felt so torn by what she was supposed to do. As a Christian, was this the right way for her to handle this?

Her eyes burning, she headed toward the bathroom to wash her face. When she walked out into the hall she found Seth standing in the open front doorway. The look on his face told her that he'd heard at least some of her conversation and there was absolutely no doubt that he knew the dampness on her face was tears…

The last thing Seth expected when he'd walked onto the porch was to overhear a personal telephone conversation between Melody and someone he'd instantly disliked.

"H-hello," she said, trying unsuccessfully to brush away her tears.

"Hi," he said, uncertain how to proceed. On the one hand, he hadn't liked the sound of the one-sided conversation or the fact that it left her in tears. On the other hand, he was reminding himself that it wasn't his business. He pointed over his shoulder with his thumb. "I was in the neighborhood and thought I'd drop in." It was lame but the only thing he had.

She remained frozen in the hallway. "Have you been standing there very long?"

He nodded, seeing humiliation in her eyes and

hating that his presence might cause her to feel that. "A few minutes. Do you want me to go? This a bad time?" *Stupid question.*

She looked away, brushing her cheeks again. Her shoulders lifted as she took what he figured was a fortifying breath. His gut twisted watching her. When she looked back she gave a tiny smile that didn't reach her eyes and shook her head.

He didn't believe her for one minute and wanted to tell her not to put on a brave front for him. Instead he watched her brow crinkle as she made an effort not to look upset. He felt like an intruder as she finally moved toward him.

"I guess you've come to ask me to leave again?"

There was none of the spunk that he'd witnessed the day before, and he missed it. Even though he wanted her off the property, there was no way he could ask her to leave when she looked so shaken. "No. I haven't changed my mind about you being here and what your research could do to my peace of mind—"

"It wouldn't cause problems."

"Yes," he said, without force, not wanting to stress her out more. "It could. But, I've decided that I'll read those journals again for myself."

She looked confused. "You want to take the journals?"

"No. That's not what I meant."

"You want to read them *with* me?"

More than he wanted to admit. "Yes." The smile that exploded across her face startled him and took his breath.

"I think that's a wonderful idea. *Please,* come in." She stepped back to give him room to enter. "I—I could actually use the company—I mean I would love to share—I mean…I started reading the journals last night, and they're really fascinating! But I do have some questions."

He was totally blown away by how swiftly the light came into her eyes, chasing away most of the shadows. Looking at her he felt bad about having an ulterior reason for wanting to read with her.

He paused just inside the doorway, unsure if he should proceed now. The stagecoach house had a straight shot from the front door to the back door. The hall walls were lined with old black-and-white photos of people from the past. Seth had always been drawn to them. He glanced at them now as he tried to figure out whether he should go or stay.

"These photos intrigue me," Melody said, nodding toward one of the pictures near the kitchen door. "This one especially." It was of a woman who'd probably never had her photo taken before and may have never had it taken again.

"I never thought she looked very happy to be in the picture," he said, moving to stand beside Melody, knowing he wasn't going anywhere—at least not for a little while. He stared closely at the picture. "Growing up, when I'd look at all these shots I wondered why none of them were smiling." He gave her a rueful glance. "I was too young to realize that to them seeing a camera was a monumental and serious thing."

"I know," Melody said, her voice as soft as the delicate floral scent she was wearing. "It was such a different world."

She touched the glass with her fingertips, leaning in slightly, as if trying to figure out what the woman was thinking. Seth was wondering what she was thinking. More intrigued by Melody than ever, he couldn't help but wonder who had been on the other end of that phone conversation and how much of it he'd missed. He had a feeling right now she was using him and the pictures as a diversion to take her mind off the upsetting call. He was sure that it was still on her mind. Again, he told himself it was none of his business, but that didn't stop him from wondering.

"Do you have any idea who this is?"

As she asked the question, she looked up at him

and caught him staring at her. Momentarily Seth lost his train of thought. "Um. No." He forced his attention back to the pictures. "Some of the other photos have captions written on the back. Someone went through and transcribed what is written on the actual photo onto the frame backing."

"I saw that." She gave him a sheepish smile. "Sorry, I peeked. I'm hoping that as I read the journals I learn more about some of them. I thought this was Jane Turner who wrote the journal I'm reading, but I'm not sure."

"She isn't my grandma Turner. We don't know who she is, but we've always wondered."

Melody studied her again. "She looks like she has a story to tell, doesn't she?"

Seth smiled. "I've always thought so."

Melody smiled, too, then led the way into the living room—it was a disaster. Seth stopped in the doorway and whistled at what he saw. The couch that had been positioned in the middle of the room was shoved against the wall along with the chair and coffee table. It had to be in order to make room for the mass of papers and books that covered the open floor space.

Melody spun at his whistle. "Oh, it's okay. I know it looks like a mess, but it really isn't. I know exactly where everything is."

He chuckled, partly because she just looked so cute standing there in the middle of the chaos. "Sure you do."

She gave a strangled laugh and turned pink. "I *do*. You don't believe me?"

He did and would have told her except he'd lost his voice. No doubt about it, he was attracted to Melody Chandler. And he was well aware that his attraction could mean problems.

"See," she stepped over a stack of books and pointed at them. "These are books on treasures and legends. *This* stack of papers are printouts of Hill Country-specific lost treasures. This one is Sam Bass-specific and these are—"

He was more stunned that she was talking so much than by the mess. Holding up a hand to halt her, he said, "I believe you." The gesture made her smile again, and knowing he'd prompted that smile made him feel unbelievably good.

"Sorry, it's just easier to have things categorized and laid open like this for easy access."

"I understand. I think." His grin widened.

She crossed her arms and studied him. "I know your type. Your desk is probably spotless. Isn't it?"

"Yeah, it is."

A shy twinkle came into her eyes. "Then come into the kitchen and sit with your back to this room so it doesn't bother you. See, I was already working in here."

He followed her to the table that was stacked with the familiar journals from the chest. He took a cane-backed chair facing the messy living room—it got him a raised eyebrow. "I'm living dangerously," he said, enjoying the teasing going on between them.

They stared at each other for a moment, and then Melody took the seat across from him. She was nervous…he made her nervous. *Everyone* made her nervous, if her usual quietness and introversion was any indication.

"I would offer you something to drink, but I wouldn't advise doing so here at the table. These are too valuable to chance a spill."

"First you call me a neat freak, and now you're calling me clumsy." He cocked his brow and watched her turn beet-red.

"*No!* I just meant, well, I'm not drinking here either."

"So just because you're messy and clumsy, you think I am?"

She chuckled, and it did his heart good to hear it. Any of the shadows that had been left from the telephone conversation had disappeared. He wasn't sure what he was doing, but all he knew was this soft-spoken woman didn't need to look sad…or stressed like she'd looked earlier.

She pulled a leather-bound journal closer to her. "These are really interesting. Did you know that Doc Holliday was reported to have stopped here?"

He nodded. "Yeah, I knew that. He was on his way from Dallas heading toward Colorado."

"So you really have read these?"

"Yes, a long time ago, but *that* story was also one of my great-great-great-great-great-grandfather's favorite campfire stories. He loved a good campfire story, and they've been passed down through the years."

Her eyes grew big. "How could you not think this place has historical value?"

"I never said I didn't think it had historical value. All I said was I own it, and I don't want it overrun with outsiders. I have special memories of my own here, and I don't care to share them with the world."

She bit her lip, studying him hard. "I just don't get you."

He laughed. "Hey, you're the history teacher. We see things differently. I think the world will do just fine without one more stagecoach house with a plaque nailed to it."

She was looking cutely perturbed at his statement when the phone rang. One ring was all it took for her to pale.

Even if he hadn't seen her earlier he'd have known something was wrong. On the second ring, she glanced across the room at the phone.

"You want me to get that?"

"No, um, I'll get it." She picked up the cordless phone and looked at the digital face. "If you'll excuse me, I'll take this…out. In the other room." She hurried from the kitchen and headed down the hall.

"Hello."

Her hushed tone carried to him, but because of the rain he couldn't make out anything more as her footsteps receded toward the back bedroom—but it wasn't because he didn't try. Politically incorrect maybe, but then he'd never been accused of being a PC kind of guy. He'd seen Melody's strained expression and heard the less than enthusiastic way she'd said hello. It had to be the same caller.

He tried to remember if he'd ever seen her with any of the local cowboys, but he didn't think so. But his first thought was that maybe he and even the fellas down at the diner had missed something—maybe she did have a love life…and maybe there was trouble in paradise.

Again, none of his business.

Picking up the journal in front of him, he flipped it open and started reading—more like he stared at the pages. The man in him, the tried-and-true cowboy, was only thinking about the tears in her eyes earlier and the look on her face just now when the phone rang.

He was a fixer. A man of action. Sitting here doing nothing was just not cuttin' it for him. But the woman would think he was crazy if he stormed in there and took over her phone call…

## Chapter Four

"Are you okay?"

"I'm fine," Melody said and prayed she looked fine. She certainly didn't feel fine. She felt like such a failure. She'd just managed to tell her brother once more that he needed to get help or she couldn't send him the money…but she knew she wouldn't hold out much longer. The conversation had been horrible. She took a deep breath. Feeling Seth watching her closely, she was determined to appear normal. He'd already seen her crying and would think he had a basket case living out here.

"So, I see you've started reading," she said, not only trying to change the subject but needing very much something else to focus on. The way he was studying her, with eyes that said he saw more than she was comfortable with him seeing, made her all the more determined to appear natural. It was a trait she'd learned growing up when Ty was making home life horrible and her parents expected her to act in public as if everything was just fine.

It was only that Seth looked concerned for her, and it touched her.

But she wasn't used to dragging her family matters out into the open. The fact that he'd seen tears in her eyes earlier couldn't be helped, but she didn't have to explain herself—not that it wouldn't be nice to have someone to talk to sometimes.

No—she was crazy to even consider talking to Seth. Shoving everything aside, she resumed reading where she'd left off and felt relief when Seth did the same.

"So, tell me why you suddenly got this idea to do all this research," he said a heartbeat later.

She looked up. "I'm a history buff, as I'm sure you've figured out," she said, grateful for the question. "And I've been teaching Texas history for the last three years. That combined with the fact that I didn't have anything to do for the summer…I came up with this idea to do research. I mean, I was living where all this unrecovered treasure is supposed to be buried. Of course, I had no idea this treasure—" she swept her hand to indicate the house "—was sitting out here until I started researching Hill Country stage stops." Melody was surprised how easy it was to talk to Seth. She was still a little uncomfortable around him, but the fact that he'd come here today interested in her work had gone a long way in easing that tension. Odd, though, since he'd seen her tears.

"So that's when you called my brother," Seth said, his voice a low drawl.

"No. Technically I called you. And believe me it took more guts than—" What was she saying? Her thoughts were crazy.

"Guts, huh? So you thought I was a bully before I drove out here and acted like one."

"*No.*" How could she tell him she didn't want to call because he was Seth Turner? The man was "sweet" as her students would say. Not "sweet" as in nice, but "sweet" as in "sweet to look at." On the other hand, with his dark hair, lean angular features and smolderingly intense eyes, "sweet" might not be the right term. The small scar at his temple only added a bit of danger.

"No?" He raised a brow.

Was he upset? "I didn't know you were a bully—" Oh, what was she *saying?* "Oh, goodness, that's not what I meant."

His eyes crinkled, and he started to chuckle. Which made her laugh because he was laughing and suddenly everything seemed surreal and unbelievable. She, Melody Chandler, was sharing this moment with Seth Turner…and she liked him. There was just no way not to. "I meant I'm just shy. Okay. Calling you up took guts."

"Oh, it did, did it?" He leaned back in his chair, hooking a arm over the back of the chair.

He looked totally relaxed and completely wonderful. Her mouth went dry. "For me," she croaked. "Because it was me being assertive."

"Now *that* I can believe." His gaze settled on her fingers where she was unconsciously still rubbing the leather corner of the journal.

Melody's insides went soft—*er* when he looked at her with a flirtatious light in his eyes…no, phooey. That was total nonsense on her part. If the look could happen to be misconstrued as flirtatious, it was simply out of total sympathy. The man knew she'd been having some kind of trouble; he was just too much of a gentleman to be nosy! She was getting sympathy smiles. Humiliating, yes, but today she was taking diversion any way she could get it!

Seth was getting off course a bit. He was here to study history, not Melody. "So you've shelved your own research for now and are zeroing in on these?"

"I'm doing both—Jane's journals could hold the clues I need in my research. My main interest is with all these millions of dollars supposedly hidden across Texas. I mean, the very *idea* is startling. But when you think about how easy it would be for someone to have come across hidden money years ago and it never got accounted for— I can't help but feel that the amount is off base. Especially where Sam Bass is concerned—the outlaw's fame has just been stretched to the hilt."

"And why is that?" Seth asked, holding back on telling her again that her interest in the money was where their problems began. But she mystified him. Again, talking about the treasure, she was blossoming right before his very eyes.

She sat up straight, energy flowing from her. "Accounts of his success and failure don't match up. And since many of his escapades happened in this area of Texas, I thought it would be fun to try and match some of the fiction with fact. That's why I'm so excited about these journals. I've realized that they may hold the key. If indeed he did rob one of these stagecoaches, if Jane wrote about it, then it very well could be a story that could expose new light on one of the *questionable* stories."

The fire was back. He found himself almost caught up in her enthusiasm. "Going through the journals might get in the way. Might slow you down if there doesn't happen to be anything like that in them."

"Oh, no! No. They're remarkable. Actually, I can't stop reading them. They're fascinating. And did you know that someone in your family started studying them? I found a couple of notes between the pages."

"I know my mom and all the grandmothers have read them."

"If so, I just don't understand. I mean, Jane has a beautiful way with words. I would think they would have realized the value of what you have here and would want to share these…" Her voice trailed off and her gaze sharpened as she searched his. He looked away—the classic sign that he was hiding something.

"Ahh," she said. "I get it. You aren't the first *male* Turner who didn't want outsiders getting their eyes on these!"

He looked back at her unapologetically. "My dad and grandfathers shared my love of the peaceful life. My mom and grandmothers understood."

"That's just wrong."

"To you. Not to me and my family."

She frowned. "You make me want to read the

journals as quickly as possible with all this secrecy. What is in these journals that y'all don't want to get out?"

It was his turn to frown.

She tapped the table with her index finger, thinking. "It couldn't be a horrible family secret in them because if there was, then the women of the family would have had a problem with showing them, too."

He kept his mouth shut. She scooted to the edge of her seat, looking like a cat about to pounce as she tried to come up with her own answers. Her eyes were alive, and he could see her mind working double-time. He'd already mentioned his grandpa Oakley's love of a good campfire tale to her. Watching her, he found himself almost tempted to tell her about granddad's favorite of all tall tales. But that was suicide—

"What is it that you're not telling me?"

Her point-blank question caused a knee-jerk laugh from him. "*Woman,* where did you come from?"

Her heart-shaped mouth curved up on one side and, like she'd been doing, she surprised him with a quick comeback. "Katy, Texas."

He grinned—couldn't help it. "You know what I mean. Here I thought you were a mouse of a woman, and you're really a tiger when you find something you want."

Her smile faded instantly and her vibrant violet eyes dulled—instantly he knew he'd said something wrong.

"Hold on, I'm sorry," he said. "That didn't come out right."

She took a deep breath and picked up a pair of dark-purple reading glasses. "No need to apologize," she said, settling the glasses firmly in place like a barrier between them. "We all have more than one side to us."

There was a chill in her words as she blinked accusingly at him from behind her glasses. He was a jerk, she said without words—but he heard her loud and clear.

*The man called her a mouse!*

The comment stung so badly that Melody couldn't look at him and looked instead to the journal. So she was shy. So she didn't stand up for herself very well…something she'd actually done yesterday with him and on the phone with Ty just now, too, after a fashion. Still, that didn't matter— the cowboy needed better manners. A man didn't go around calling a woman a mouse…even if he was complimenting her in a strange sort of way.

Nobody had to tell her she was a mouse! She knew it better than anyone.

The clock in the room ticked the seconds by as she pretended to study the journal in front of her. She had found herself enjoying the banter. It was so totally not her that it had been refreshing. And it had been such a welcome distraction from her troubles with Ty.

So much so that she'd almost forgotten that no way in the world was Seth Turner flirting with her…and *she* hadn't been flirting with him either. Had she? How embarrassing.

She blinked and stared at the page harder. Why didn't he just go home and let her work? She'd had a bad morning, her equilibrium was off, obviously—that explained her uncharacteristic behavior where Seth was concerned. But now would be a perfect time for him to leave.

Only *now*, she seemed to have reverted back to mousehood and didn't feel comfortable asking him to go.

But she was going to. She was going to make herself or else. "You—"

"You know," he said at the same time. "Sorry, you go ahead."

"No. That's okay. You go."

"I'm expecting a load of cattle to be delivered,

so I'm going to go and get out of your hair. I didn't mean to insult you. I've enjoyed this talk."

He stood and she did, too. "You didn't hurt my feelings. Really. It has been a bit of a stressful day for me. Sorry if I acted badly." It was true, and there was no pretending that he didn't know something was going on with the phone.

"You don't have any reason to apologize. Look," he said, but halted as if he'd lost his train of thought as he stared at her.

And why not, because she was crazy. His simple denial that she didn't have anything to apologize for had her blinking hard against tears and there was no way he couldn't tell it! He probably thought something was mentally wrong with her.

"Are you okay?" he asked.

She nodded but couldn't look at him. He touched her arm, and she couldn't help the sharp intake of breath from his unexpected touch. Her gaze flew as sharply to meet his. "You are welcome to stop by anytime," she blurted and stepped away.

"Thanks," he said, turned on his boot and was gone.

Melody followed him to the door and watched as he jogged through the rain that was turning from a light downpour into a torrential mess… Melody actually welcomed the storm.

She closed the front door and went to the kitchen and started cooking brownies. There were many things in life she couldn't understand or control but brownies she knew.

# Chapter Five

Seth hadn't lied about cattle arriving. "Hey, Dan," he shouted over the thunder. "Sorry I'm late." He'd pulled his oilskin duster from beneath the seat and tugged it on as he stomped through the water washing across the rock drive. Dan, his good friend and neighbor, hauled cattle for a living—he was also the local horseshoer and raised his own herd, too.

"No problem," he said. He'd backed his large hauler up to the corral and was opening the gate. "You know I don't actually need you out here in this. No sense both of us getting soaked."

"I know." Seth tugged his collar up against the driving rain and stood out of the way. Dan knew what he was doing and often when he arrived from a long haul unloaded by himself. But there was always the chance that something could go wrong, and it didn't take but one slipup and even the most experienced of cowboys could get slammed or stomped. "How's Ashby feeling?" Seth asked. The cattle began unloading, and Dan came to stand beside him.

"She's the happiest pregnant woman I've ever seen. Even when she was throwing her guts up the woman was smiling." He chuckled. "She wanted a baby so bad even being so sick isn't fazing her. Beats all I ever saw. She's special. You need to find you a good woman. I'm telling you, especially on a night like tonight…" he didn't finish but his happy expression said everything that needed to be said.

"I guess I'll just have to settle for a hot cup of coffee and the news."

"Man, you gotta get a life."

"I thought you were saying I needed a wife."

"Hey, bro. It's the same thing."

"We aren't all as lucky in love as you, my man."

Dan hiked a dark brow and let all his pearly whites shine through the rain. "Now didn't you learn nothin' from watching me chase that poor woman down until she had no choice but to agree to marry my sorry hide? Luck had nothing to do with it. Oh, no. It was pure, hard-nosed determination on my part, and the good Lord taking pity on me, that got that little woman to give me the time of day, much less to marry me."

"Yeah, I know that's the truth." Seth chuckled.

Dan headed off to pull the gate closed behind the herd. The cocky cowboy was one of the best-natured and most good-hearted cowboys Seth had ever met. And he spoke the truth about how hard he'd worked to get his wife to even give him a second glance. Seth wondered how that would feel. He dated. He even thought he was serious a time or two, but in the end things just fizzled and he'd been okay with that by that point. He hadn't had a date in six months. Maybe that was why he'd suddenly gotten this unexpected attraction to his new tenant.

Melody had slept amazingly well. Storms always seemed to work like a lullaby for her. For as long as she could remember, her last thought before she went to bed at night was of Ty. And her first waking thought was of him. She said her prayer for him automatically as she climbed out of bed and headed for her morning coffee. It was a new day. If she continued saying no to the money he asked for, he very well could be evicted. She knew he'd been lying to her for several months, and the money she'd believed he was using to pay his rent and utilities had actually gone to pay for his drug habit.

He was ruled by his addictions and didn't care an ounce if she went into debt to pay for his drug habit so long as he still got his fix. She'd been horrified when her parents had been killed in the car accident. That had been compounded by her discovery that they'd died deeply in debt from money they'd borrowed against their home and credit cards. And all the money had gone to fund Ty's lifestyle.

*Enough!*

She finished her coffee and headed to get ready for the day. She was throwing herself into her work today. To say she'd been distracted the day before was an understatement. Today, hopefully, there would be none of that.

She was disappointed by noon when she'd found nothing about stagecoach robberies in the three journals she was reading. As fascinating as the writing was, she was disappointed as she went back to the chest. She was on her knees reaching into the chest for the last two journals when a board inside the very back corner of the closet caught her attention. It was crooked slightly, and from where she was sitting on the floor it looked like it wasn't nailed. Abandoning the chest, she scooted inside the closet and ran her fingers over the board. It moved.

But didn't come out of its slot. Curious, she went to the kitchen and got a butter knife. Returning to the closet she dropped to her knees and inserted the tip of the knife into the crack and pried. Instantly the short board popped from the wall, exposing a small space between the closet wall and the kitchen wall behind it. And inside the cavity was a leather-bound journal.

Seth was coming out of his barn carrying a chainsaw when Melody's car came careening dangerously over his cattle guard.

"What's wrong?" he asked, hurrying to the car and yanking open the door.

She stumbled out in an instant clutching one of the journals against her. "Y-you aren't going to believe this! I found a map!"

Seth caught her as she almost tripped over her feet. Her face was lit up like fireworks on the Fourth of July. Her eyes glowed, and her smile was so explosive that Seth didn't catch what she was saying at first. "A what?"

"*A treasure map!*" she said, grabbing his arm and dragging him toward his porch to enter the house. "There was a board in the closet and it was loose. Behind it was this journal—it was just in there. And I pulled it out and started reading but then this fell out and it was all there."

"Whoa, hold up." She was babbling ninety miles an hour as she placed the journal on the table and opened it. Inside was a folded piece of paper, which she carefully opened. It wasn't a map drawn like one thought of a typical map. Instead it was a handwritten list. Seth couldn't help the rush of adrenaline that he got looking at it. Was this proof that his granddad's campfire tale was true? He pulled up a chair and Melody did the same as he read it.

"Begin south corner ravine at the matching rocks. Fifty steps west to tower turn twenty-five degrees left. At the rock follow the crust to the cave."

His heart was pounding as he met Melody's big eyes. "Who wrote this?"

"Jane."

Seth told himself to breathe.

Melody pointed to the familiar writing inside the journal. It was the same clear, precise writing as the others. "She says here that on May 5, 1877, not long after they'd moved to the stage stop, they were awakened in the middle of the night by a sound. When Oakley went to investigate he found a very sick man. They took him in and tried to help

him but the man died two days later. But in his
fever, he told your Grandpa Oakley where he'd
hidden three saddlebags of gold coins."

The campfire tale. "Does it say who he was?
Where this money came from?"

Melody beamed. "Not so far as I've read. And
there is absolutely no telling. Do you even have
any idea how many stage robberies and train robberies took place between 1874 and 1878? Many
of them. And that's what I've been telling you.
See, it got crazy during that time—and Sam Bass
was accused of committing most of the crimes.
But to have done everything he is credited for
doing he would have had to be ten men. No way
could he have done everything he was accused of.
So, that's the deal, there were men roaming
around out there who robbed things and never got
caught. It was a perfect time to be a robber with
all the well-known gangs wreaking havoc on the
territories stretching from Nebraska to Texas. This
sick man could have been anyone and the money
could have come from who knows what holdup!
And, of course, I haven't read this entire journal.
I was too excited to come show you first, but so
far there's no name or anything. I'm thinking there
won't be. If that's so, we may never know who
this guy was."

Seth stared at her. "Man, you know your stuff."

"Oh, there is just so much to know. It is fascinating."

He smiled. "But you really like this."

That stumped her. "Well, yes. I love it. I mean, I've always loved history, and I used to think it would even be fun to search for treasures, but well, there really wasn't an opportunity. But we can now. Isn't that exciting?"

"Wait. You mean actually look for this?"

"Well, sure."

"No."

She blinked and reared back as if he'd hit her. "But, it's right there." She tapped the map. "Written out. You must look for it."

There was a part of him that was excited beyond measure, but he had a practical side and it kicked in. As did his wary side. He was looking at his worst fear…yes this very well could be his great-grandfather's campfire tale, and that meant if word of this got out he could kiss his peace and quiet goodbye.

Still, there was a part of him that wanted to grab the map, grab Melody and head for the ravine in search of lost treasure. "Look, Melody. I really don't want this getting out. I'd rather you said nothing to anyone about this. You said it yourself there might be no way of knowing who this mystery man was. Or where the money came from. I don't want word getting out that this is here or the loonies will come. Do you see what I'm saying?"

She was looking at him like he had two heads. "You don't mean that you really want to pretend I didn't just find this."

"That's exactly what I want."

"No *way*—you have to say something about this."

"No. I don't," he said emphatically.

"Wait. Look at what's copied here. Do you have any idea what some of these things mean?"

"The guy's talking about my ravine. But I have no idea what the other stuff is. Do you have any idea how big that area is?"

"No. Take me to see it."

"Melody. Be rational here. Yes, we have a map. But the ravine is a massive area. There are streams, and its several hills all run together, densely wooded, too. Me and my brothers camped there growing up, and it's great for hunting and fishing. But I've never seen a cave. Not that we didn't think there might be one. We did, but if there is one, it is so well hidden that we never ran across it nor did anyone else in my family or they'd surely have passed down that they had. If this dead guy found it by accident and buried treasure in it then he was one lucky guy."

"It could happen," she huffed, crossing her arms.

She wasn't listening. Her mind was on the treasure. "So you're saying he just happened to be riding across the land, sick, found this cave accidentally, hid the treasure then came here and died. It's too convenient. And even if it did happen like that the odds of us coming across it are—"

"—highly improved because we now have a map! Come on, Seth. At least show me what we're talking about. Please."

He sighed. The mouse had turned into a bulldog—though she was way too pretty to be compared to a short, snub-nosed creature. He figured the best way to dissuade her was to show her. "Come on, get in my truck," he said. She startled him all the more by rewarding him with a jubilant hug.

Ever since she'd discovered the map, she hadn't been able to think properly. Her brain was in overdrive. She wanted to surge full throttle ahead on this adventure. But Seth was forcing the parking brake. When he'd agreed to show her the ravine, hugging him had just happened. She didn't throw her arms around men in ecstatic hugs—this was not who or what she did. But, then, she realized as they rode through his pastures that she didn't mind so much not being who she'd always been.

She was going to hunt for this treasure. She was. All she had to do was convince Seth to help her. It would be *so* much fun.

They drove about five miles cross-country through the flat pastures then up into the hills and the trees. When he brought the truck to a stop at last, they were sitting at the top of a ravine. Before her was a vast, deep, densely wooded swath of steep hills and gullies. She was amazed at how quickly the terrain could change here in the hill country.

"*Now* do you see what I've been trying to explain? If this guy accidentally found a cave, the odds that he got the map right are against him. You can get turned around in there even when you know the lay of the land as well as I do."

She could believe that. Looking at the scope of the ravine made the task appear almost impossible. *Almost*. She would not be denied as she looked at Seth and smiled. "But we have a map."

## Chapter Six

"So does anything around here look like twins to you? I mean you said you've been all around out here. It's probably something easy."

Seth climbed over a large fallen tree trunk and held his hand out to Melody. Treasure on his land was the last thing he wanted, but he didn't mind hiking through the woods with Melody. She was not an outdoorsy kind of woman but she was trying, probably because she was so excited. He hated to tell her that her excitement wasn't going to make him decide to go any farther than this short trip. He was indulging her for a minute just to dissuade her, but he had no intention of opening this potential hornet's nest. He was just trying to show her how futile it would be to search out here.

Still, he was feeling guilty about it when she smiled like a schoolgirl and took his outstretched hand. A jolt of electricity shot through him, and she immediately stumbled over the tree trunk as her eyes locked with his, making him think she felt it, too. He swallowed hard and tried to concentrate.

There was no denying the fact that if he didn't focus on the big picture he could very well lose his head and do something stupid. "So do you see anything?" he asked again.

"You mean matching rocks?" she asked.

"Right. That's what I mean," he said, more harshly than he should have. "You ever been walking around in the woods?"

Her expression turned wistful. "No. Katy's a bit more city than this, being so tied in with the Houston area. But I'll get used to it. I'm a bookworm, remember?" She glanced back at him.

He had to react quickly, thrusting a tree limb out of her way before she ran into it. "Believe me, I've noticed."

"But, I've thought about it. I've even thought it would be fun to hike down into the Grand Canyon."

That made him laugh. "Sorry. But that's a bit ambitious for a gal who doesn't even get out into the woods every once in awhile."

She deflated. "Well, it's just something I've

thought about." She looked around, then beamed. "And I'm out here now. That's a start."

Man, the woman was just too cute. "Yes, it is. I'm the one who's out here under duress."

She didn't smile, but he could see her eyes crinkle up at the edges. It was a nice day, and even if he had no expectations for where this was going, he definitely could go along with her for awhile. She was having a good time. And the woman most surely needed to get out more.

She shielded her eyes as she scanned the ravine. "So, what do you think he meant by the matching rocks? It has to be something prominent. I mean, he was just riding through, so to him it had to be an easy landmark."

He scratched his neck and gave it some real thought. "I have two different thoughts." He checked his watch. It was three o'clock and wouldn't start getting dark for a few hours, so they could at least hike to the rock outcropping.

"Then lead on," she said, slapping at a buffalo gnat. Seth grabbed her elbow when she subsequently stepped in a hole.

"Steady there."

"Thanks. So, tell me about your grandfather," she said as he held a branch out of the way so she could move forward.

"Which one?"

"Oakley. The one who won this land in a poker game—he's the one who hid this map. He sounded like a card."

"Oh, he was that. Not the most upstanding citizen from what we know." He glanced back at her and lifted a brow. "We think he may have considered riding with one of those gangs in his day. That's the kind of guy he was."

"He wouldn't have been alone. Do you know that in that decade of the 1870s a lot of cowboys considered it?"

"Yeah, but that doesn't make it right."

She laughed. "Well, no, I didn't say it was right. I'm just saying that was a fact of the times. It's part of the reason for so much folklore and admiration that was felt for some of those outlaws."

"Didn't Sam Bass help poor folks out by giving them cash?"

She shrugged. "Who knows? There are so many accounts. Some say he never took money from the people on the stagecoaches, but that's not true. He had no problem hurting the train porters. He beat one unconscious with the butt of his pistol when the guy couldn't tell him the safe combination."

"Not a good thing."

She studied the ravine again. "Just imagine, a

treasure could be hidden right out there. Practically in your backyard."

"Big whoop."

"Why are you such a sourpuss when it comes to this buried treasure? Crazies are not going to come here. Relax. Besides, with a scowl like that, if they did come, they'd take one look at you and run."

"That'd be the smart move for them to make."

Melody balled her fists on her hips and looked at him like she didn't know what to think about him. Well, that was two of them.

"What year did your grandfather win all of this in the poker game? And, by the way, that is really curious to me."

"What's *not* curious to you?"

"Hey, you should try being curious some time—like now. Don't you find it odd that someone would risk all of this in a poker game? Goodness, how bad do you have to be to want to risk losing this much?"

"Um, gamblers have a problem with limiting themselves," he said, arching a brow. "That's why they're called *gamblers*."

She rolled her violet eyes.

"No. He didn't win all of this in a poker game," he conceded. "He won seventy acres, is all, and brought his family here to take over running the stage stop. His son married the only child of the man who owned the rest of the land."

"Do you realize that you and your brothers know more about your ancestors seven generations back than most people know about one generation back? I mean goodness, Seth—you're talking about your great-grandfather's great-great-grandfather!"

"We tend to take it for granted," he started walking again but she lagged behind. He glanced back at her. "You coming or you going to stand there in the bushes?"

"Sorry, I just think it's fascinating. How do you know so much?"

"The campfire stories. See, the thing is that some of what we know we're sure is true. But the problem is much of what we know is also likely pure fabrication. We come from a long line of…to put it politely, storytellers."

"So, are you and your brothers storytellers?" she asked. He turned to answer her just as the dirt shifted under her feet and suddenly she was in his arms.

He steadied her but didn't release her—he'd be telling a story right then if he denied that he really wanted to kiss Melody Chandler. She was sweet and amazingly beautiful—he was still baffled at how he'd missed that. It wasn't in the classic sense of the word but it was deeper, in the look in her eyes and the texture of her skin. The warmth of her smile and that touch of humor and shyness that battled against the fire he couldn't get out of his head…he dropped his hand and stepped back.

He willed his head to clear. "Wyatt's more of the storyteller. Cole is a little bit."

She smoothed her hair and said softly, "But not you. You're the serious one."

"You could say that. Look, we're almost there. Come on."

What was he doing? He wasn't going to actually hunt for this treasure, was he? When she had realized that—well, it was safe to say he wasn't going to be one of her favorite people. Coming out here in the first place had been a mistake.

They walked in silence for a minute. He marched ahead of her, lost in battle with himself over what to do.

"Do you and your brothers get along?"

"Usually," he drawled, cocking a brow over his shoulder at her.

She grimaced. "Meaning me. My being here is a problem between you?" She stopped walking. "I really wouldn't want to cause hard feelings between you."

True, he didn't like Wyatt's little stunt or the fact that he'd pulled a disappearing act and wasn't answering his phone. But their brotherly bond was strong and he didn't feel right making Melody think her presence was straining their relationship. "You're not so bad," he said, then hopped up on a large rock and held his hand out to her.

"It's really not a problem?" she asked. Taking his hand, she scrambled up beside him with his help.

They were standing close, and their proximity suddenly seemed more intimate than it should. Seth let go of her hand. "No problem. But," he warned, "if you go telling that you found a treasure map I'm not going to be so fond of you."

"But—"

"Nope. Not a word. Or the deal is off. Now, turn around and tell me what you think. This might be the outcropping we're looking for."

She didn't look at first, instead turned a distracting shade of pink, the color of a dawn…his favorite time of day. His gaze dropped to her lips—he immediately reminded himself that she was not a sunrise and this was not the direction he'd planned to go when he'd brought her out here.

Melody's head was about to explode from everything that she had going on inside of it. She was looking for a buried treasure—with a gorgeous man! And she'd just gotten the distinct impression that that gorgeous man had just been thinking about kissing her…no, surely not. This was Seth Turner and she was a mouse—he'd said so himself.

It was a ridiculous thought on her part. Feeling foolish, she carefully turned away from Seth, making sure she didn't topple off the large rock they were standing on. What she saw filled her with such excitement she almost lost her balance and only Seth's hand on her waist stopped her fall. "Look," she gasped. Two rocks could be seen about fifty feet down the side of the hill. They were about as tall as her, and though they didn't look exactly the same, they did look like a pair.

"This could be it!" she exclaimed, glancing over her shoulder at him. He smiled and his hand on her waist tightened.

"Steady there," he said.

She looked back toward the rocks, telling herself the interest she saw in his eyes was her imagination and she needed to be very careful. Seth Turner wouldn't find a plain woman like her attractive. He was the type of man who would not only date gorgeous women but also dynamic, self-confident women. A mousy history teacher like her was not in his league and she knew it. To let him realize she was thinking about him in that way would be embarrassing. She was a practical girl after all…on a treasure hunt! At least that made her feel better.

"Can we go down there?" she asked, filled with anticipation. That was what had her head crazy—it was the excitement of the map. Otherwise she would never have been entertaining such thoughts about Seth.

"Not today. We won't make it back to the truck before nightfall."

"But it's right there."

"Melody, we'd have to climb down that steep rocky incline, and then we still wouldn't have time to get any farther with the map instructions. I'm telling you, it's too late."

"But—"

"Hey, no discussion. I brought you out here to show it to you. That's it. And you're lucky I did that."

Melody bit her tongue. The man was intent on reminding her that he didn't want to have anything to do with this treasure. She was fuming as he hopped to the ground and held his arms up to her. "I can get down from here by myself," she snapped, grabbing a tree branch to steady herself and proceeding to slip and slide down the rock.

Seth watched her with a grimace, and she felt

foolish for having not taken his helping hands. Especially when she could see her actions had him secretly wanting to laugh!

Humiliated, she scooted past him and kept on walking. She'd show him that she could hike through the woods with the best of them. As a matter of fact, she'd be back out here tomorrow, and she was going to really start looking for the treasure. She'd show him all right. She should thank him for bringing her out here and showing her the way. But she didn't. She wasn't stupid, and if he didn't want to hunt for the treasure that was his problem.

"Are you mad at me?" he asked, falling into step beside her as she plowed back the way they'd come.

"I hardly have the right to be mad at you. This is your property after all. Your map. Your treasure."

He was staring at her. She could tell even though she didn't dare take her eyes off the path—at the rate she was going, to do so would be pure stupidity. But he was watching her, and she knew because the hair on the back of her neck was standing up. She glared back at him. "I can't believe you brought me out here to yank my chain, to—to dangle the treasure hunt in front of my eyes. You never had any intention of looking for the treasure. Jerk!" She continued stomping uphill.

"Melody, c'mon. I'm sorry. I didn't mean it that way. I was trying to show you how futile it would be. Please slow down. At this rate you could break your neck. There are all sorts of holes—"

"I'm not going to step in a hole," she barked. "You think I can't even walk around out here by myself? Well, I can."

He *chuckled.* "Don't laugh at me," she warned, walking faster—stumbling.

"Melody, I'm sorry I laughed. You just surprised me with your temper. And I never said you couldn't hike. Would you hold up?"

He apologized twice, but she was too mad to care. "*You're* the one who said it was going to get dark soon. You know you've just laid out all the rules. Why is it that *everyone* in my life sets the rules that I'm supposed to follow? *Everyone* thinks that they can just tell me what I'm supposed to do and that little ole Melody will just do it! Well, look, buster, I can at least hike through the woods without someone telling me—" Melody halted in her tracks. What was she doing? What had she just said? Her hand clamped over her mouth, and she lifted mortified eyes to Seth.

His expression was concerned. "You want to explain some of that?"

She shook her head. What she wanted was for the earth to open and swallow her up.

"At the risk of being one of those who tells you what to do…I think it might be a good idea."

*Chapter Seven*

"Why don't you come in?" Seth said when he pulled to a stop in front of his house.

"I think I'll go home. But thank you," Melody said, reaching for the journal and the map. He'd been quiet the entire drive from the ravine—and so had she. But it didn't take much to see that something was bothering him. Something was on his mind. She just wasn't sure if it was treasure hunting or if he was thinking about her outburst. How had her emotions twisted like that? It was such an accusatory statement…somehow in her frustration at him over telling her she couldn't hunt for treasure she'd brought her personal life into the mix.

"Can I ask you a personal question?" he asked, his voice gentle, as if worried she'd have another temper tantrum.

She wanted to crawl under a rock. She did not want to answer a personal question. Oh, how she wished he wouldn't ask, but how could she say that? "I guess," she said instead.

"Do you have a boyfriend?"

"A boyfriend?" Her heart lunged into her throat. Where had that come from?

"Yeah, or someone who takes you out on occasion?"

The wind was rushing in her ears, only the wind wasn't blowing. Had she been right earlier? She'd thought her aloneness in the dating horizon was pretty obvious. It was mortifying.

"No," she said. "No boyfriend. Wh-why?"

"If someone is bothering you, I'd like to help."

The words had her stopping in her tracks. "What?" The word came out in a squeak. This wasn't about him wanting to ask her out—could she have been any more silly for that thought to cross her mind?

"Look, I've tried to stay out of your business, but the phone calls yesterday and then your statement out there—I can't stand by and let someone harass you. That's just not the way I'm wired."

She was trembling and probably as red as the rose blooming in the flowerbed beside her. "No, I—I don't need anything." Need to hide, oh, yes—for years and years. Need to not shake and keep her eyes down because she couldn't chance him looking into them and guessing what she'd been thinking. She reached for the journal. "I have to go."

He laid his hand over hers as her fingers curled around the journal. "Talking might help."

She shook her head and tugged at the journal, her eyes riveted to the strength in his hand. Her mind wondering what it would be like to feel that touch in a caress—stop. Foolish, foolish woman.

She shook her head. She needed to go before she did something humiliating.

His hand slid from hers and curled firmly around the journal. He slid it from her grasp. "I think I'll keep this."

"What?" Now she looked at him.

"I want to read the journal tonight and decide what I want to do."

"What you're going to do? We're going to look for the treasure. We have to."

"Melody, I don't know if we are."

"But—" She was starting to sound like a broken record.

"I'm going to think about this."

Melody had felt frustrated and controlled and foolish all of her life—why should she have thought now would be any different? But this was his property. His map. His choice. Looking at Seth she wanted to scream that he had no right to take this from her. She'd found the map. But she already had him thinking she was half-crazy—that could be why he needed to think about what to do with the map. "Okay," she said, holding in her frustrations. "But please give it fair thought." That said, she hurried to her car and drove away.

"Cole, I'm telling you one last time to get on the phone, call Wyatt and tell him if he doesn't call me I'm going to hunt him down."

"Hold on, Seth." Cole's rumbled laughter came across loud and clear on the other end of the phone line. "I already told him. He called yesterday from Greece."

"Greece!"

"His partners needed him to fly over there to meet a client. He said to tell you to calm down. He'll be back in town next week. But for now he said to chill and to stop worrying about keeping people off your property and out of your life."

Seth's grip tightened. "He needs to mind his own business—"

"He's our big brother. You know how he is. Once he gets something in that head of his, he won't let it go."

"What exactly is it he's gotten into his head?"

Cole groaned, which didn't reassure Seth. Growing up, their big brother had thought it was his born duty as the firstborn to lead them whether they wanted to be led or not.

"Look, Seth, you know as well as I do that he flies by the seat of his pants. When opportunity knocks he takes it."

"Yeah, so what are you saying?"

"I think he met this Melody and he thought she was too sweet to pass up. Look, man, let her do her thing. From what he said she was a real shy case. He's a marshmallow and couldn't turn her away."

"I'll say he didn't turn her away! He moved her in, and now everything is in a mess."

"Relax, Seth—"

"Cole, she found a treasure map," he snapped.

"Get outta here! For real?"

Seth leaned back and looked up at the ceiling. "For real. It was hidden behind a slat in the hall closet and there's more. It's proof that the campfire tales had merit. Grandma Jane documented that they took in a sick man, and before he died he gave them the directions to where he hid some saddle-bags of gold coins in a cave in the ravine."

Cole laughed then let out a slow whistle as the news sank in. "Man, all those years when we were roaming that place dreaming of finding the treasure and proving the legend was true. So, what does this mean?"

Seth grunted. "That my quiet country life could turn into a circus."

"You've got to be kidding me. We're talking about a real live *treasure* hunt."

"Yeah, loonies, trespassers and jerks running amok thinking this is a green light for them."

"Now, just wait a stinkin' minute. You were the leader as a boy when we would roam those hills for treasure. Where's that kid now? I think that's what me and Wyatt have been wondering about for a while now. What happened to you, man?"

Seth rubbed his temple. "That went away with my stick horse and my pop gun."

"Yep, that's what Wyatt's talking about. You need to loosen up, and he thought this was the way to do it…he'll be as blown away as me when he finds out about this treasure map. *Now,* tell me about this map *and* the woman."

A vision of Melody played across Seth's mind. Knowing he'd let her down was eating at him, even though he'd warned her all along. But more than the treasure maps nagged at him, he had to know who had been on the end of those phone conversations that had upset her so much.

"Seth, you there?"

"Yeah, I'm here. Melody's a real nice lady. Real quiet—most of the time. Honestly, she makes you want to give her whatever she asks for. Even take her on a treasure hunt." It was the truth, and he knew it. He pushed out of his rolling desk chair so hard it shot back and hit the wall. He didn't even glance at it as he strode to the window and stared out at the darkness. He saw the shadowy shapes of a group of deer hopping the fence between the barn and open ground as they headed toward the hills.

"Then go for it. What are you waiting for? You and Melody might actually find something out there."

"And we might not. I don't have the time to just go traipsing off into the woods on a wild-goose chase. This ranch is—"

"Not going to fall apart if you take some time off. That's why you have those cowboys working for you. Now tell me what the map says."

Disgruntled all the more, Seth snagged up the map and read the list. "So, what do you make of it? What would you think the ravine with the matching rocks is? South corner. That's the start point. I took her out today and showed her the spot we used to camp at."

"That might be it. But that's not really the south corner. Maybe he was talking about the ledge."

Seth had thought about that. "Yeah, could be that. But if he was sick, it'd be hard to manage."

"You're right." Cole chuckled. "See, you're thinking about it. Come on, man, get with the program. This is fun. Dream a little. You know as well as I do that there was a time when you wanted to find a treasure map. Get out there and make your ancestors proud…at least give it a shot. And take Melody along. She sounds nice."

"She is. But something is going on with her. I'm not sure that she doesn't have a boyfriend who's giving her trouble. She told me she didn't, but I overheard her on the phone and she was really upset. And I saw her before and after another phone call, and it wasn't good. I think she's scared."

"Not good. You think a boyfriend is harassing her?"

"Can't say for sure, but I've never seen her with anyone round town. But that doesn't mean someone isn't in the picture."

"Maybe you need to stick close and find out how you can help her."

Seth had thought about that. The entire day was filled with red flags on all kinds of problems.

"Look, I'll call you later. You going to make it up for the Fourth?"

"*Maay*be." Cole dragged the word out. "I'll have to let you know next week. I might not be able to get away."

"Heard that a million times."

"Hey, you're the country boy, remember. Me, I've got places to be and people to see."

Seth hung up after saying goodbye, but he didn't head to bed. Instead he sat down and flipped back through the journal he'd been reading, his thoughts fixated on Melody.

Cole was right when he'd said they used to hunt for treasure. Seth remembered clearly how much dreaming they'd done about that treasure. It had been a long time since he'd been a kid, though. A long time since his thoughts had been on treasure hunting. Even now, it wasn't the treasure he was thinking about. It was Melody, and what was going on that had her so distressed.

How could a day so absolutely amazing and exciting end up so terribly? She was mad at Seth, mad at herself and mad at Ty…once again her brother had managed to put a spoiler on her day. Intruding when least expected.

And Seth…what was the man's problem? He

was a domineering brute! A tease. He'd dangled that ravine in front of her like a carrot—knowingly getting her hopes up. He'd apologized for leading her on, but that didn't change that he'd done it. Men. He was so clueless because he'd done it after he'd almost made her think he cared about her feelings. And after she'd almost been tempted to tell him about Ty…

At their insistence, she'd never talked with anyone but her parents about her brother. Before her parents died in the car crash, they'd always said this was a family matter and it should be handled privately. True, they'd talked with various doctors of the rehab centers Ty had been in and out of but never, ever did they talk about it with friends. Though those close to them knew there was a problem, it was just an unspoken agreement that it was not a topic of discussion. But unlike her parents, Melody knew that opinions about Ty were aired. She heard the whispers at church or heard conversations dry up as she'd entered a room. It was tiring. And though she knew she wasn't the only person out there with a drug-addicted family member it felt like she was. After attending Houston Community College in Katy and getting her degree, she went against what her parents wanted and took the job in Mule Hollow's rural school. It had hurt her parents that she'd chosen to leave Katy but she'd had to.

She'd had to distance herself from Ty. In doing so she'd hoped to never mention his name to anyone from Mule Hollow. No one even knew she had a brother…her heart clenched at the thought, but God forgive her she liked it that way. Though it hadn't really helped with the strain she felt because of him at least she didn't have to worry about people whispering behind her back. Ty put enough strain on her without having to live with everyone knowing what she was going through.

So there it was. The truth. She was an accomplished history teacher who was pretending she was someone else. Someone who didn't have a drug-addicted, alcoholic brother.

And that was exactly the way she wanted to keep it.

So why had she almost told Seth? Especially when he was the one who'd made her mad in the first place and ruined her day by causing her to think of Ty even out there in the boonies.

Calm down, sister, she told herself and took a swig of chamomile tea—she hated the stuff but her mom had believed it calmed a person down. She wasn't sure it did, but at this point she was willing to try anything.

That had been yesterday after all, and she had research to do. She took another sip of tea and almost gagged—goodness, this stuff was gross! She gave up and set the cup down. It was time to get to work…*work* would calm her. Work was where she'd find answers, and work was where she might be able to find some clue as to the identity of the man Seth's ancestors had gotten the treasure map from. If she could figure that much out, maybe Seth's curiosity would be roused more and he would agree to the treasure hunt.

Because Melody had decided something important. Yesterday, she'd turned tail and quietly given up…like the good, passive little girl she'd been taught to be. But today she knew she couldn't live with that. Nope. She couldn't…she was on the trail of a piece of American history. Goodness, a fire was burning inside her and she knew no matter what she *had* to bring out the truth. She had been given a mission…and, by George, she was going see it through.

Seth Turner was afraid the crazies would come if word of a treasure got out. And he was absolutely right, only, if he didn't get on board he was about to find out that the first crazy was already here!

## Chapter Eight

"Melody, girl—we need to talk," Lacy Matlock called as soon as Melody climbed out of her car the next morning. As usual, the little church parking lot was bulging with cars and trucks. She scanned the group and found the one she was looking for. Seth was here. As she hurried toward her friend, she checked on the various clumps of people visiting on the lawn. When she saw him standing on the edge with a group of other cattlemen, her heart did an aggravating tumble. When his gaze caught hers and held, she suddenly found it hard to breathe!

She looked away quickly—not exactly the powerhouse of determination she was shooting for.

"How've you been?" Lacy asked, giving her an exuberant hug. Lacy was the local hairstylist who'd moved to town and helped bring the dusty, dying place into the wonderful, welcoming community that it was today. When Melody had come to teach at the school Mule Hollow shared with the small rural communities she'd had to live in Ranger, which was seventy miles away. There wasn't anything to draw her to live in Mule Hollow. The schoolhouse was twenty miles from town and honestly back then the dead clapboard town was only a place cowboys could love. Sam's Diner, Pete's Feed and Seed, Prudy's Garage and not much else... But that had all changed when Norma Sue, Esther Mae and Adela, the three older ladies who loved their little town, had come up with the plan to advertise for wives for all the cowboys. Why, Melody and the other school-teachers had been so shocked to see the ad in the paper. And the next thing they knew, almost before the ink on the first ad was dry, Lacy had driven into town in her *pink* 1958 Cadillac convertible!

The exuberant hairstylist was like a tornado when she hit town. She'd come to open a salon with her friend Sheri, who was riding shotgun in the Caddy. And she'd come to help the ladies succeed in their plan to bring women to Mule Hollow. It had been amazing. Really, for a quiet gal like herself, Melody had been curious to watch what was happening. Even though she was too shy to come looking for a husband, she'd been one of the first women to move to town when Adela turned her big old home into an apartment house. But she'd watched as women came and fell in love. And now, some were even having babies. Even Lacy was trying, but so far no luck. Melody hoped it happened soon for her and Clint, though.

Several times when she'd really felt down, she'd thought about telling Lacy about her "other" life. But she always held back. "Hi. I'm in the nursery for Sunday school so I've got to head in," she said, glancing toward Seth from beneath her lowered lashes. "You want to walk with me?"

"Sure do," Lacy said, falling into step beside her. "It seems like forever since I've seen you. You did just what I thought you'd do."

"What's that?"

"You disappeared the minute you moved to the boonies." Her bluebird-colored eyes twinkled.

"I've been busy." Melody wanted more than anything to share the news about the treasure map. She felt like a kid with a dollar burning a hole in her pocket.

"I know, I know. You've buried yourself in all that research and you're swimming in happiness. But we miss you."

"I'm coming to the July Fourth planning meeting on Tuesday."

"And you're going to help with one of the booths this year, too. I'm not letting you hide in a food cart this year."

"But—"

"Nope, nope, nope. You are getting out and about this year. Two years hiding in the cotton candy trailer is just not going to cut it anymore. I'm putting you somewhere with a little more life, and there is just nothing you can do to change my mind."

They'd reached the nursery door. "Okay, I'll do whatever you want." There, she was stepping out of her comfort zone and as impulsive as Lacy was, Melody still trusted her.

"Great! The posse is getting back from their little vacation on the high seas tomorrow night so I'm going to huddle up with them, and by the time you show up Tuesday night we're going to have you all situated. Do you want to come out to the house after church for lunch?"

"I can't. I really want to get home and back to my work." Over Lacy's shoulder she saw Seth come in the annex door and head for the singles class. He looked handsome in his twill western-cut dress slacks and cream-colored blazer. The buttery tone of the jacket made his smoky eyes

pop with intensity. And her nerves jangled like a
load of bangle bracelets when their gazes met.
Despite trying not to, she was attracted to the
maddening man.

"I'll see you later," she said to Lacy and ducked
into the nursery. Chicken Little had nothing on
her. That little chicken was silly for foolishly
thinking the sky was falling…but if she fell for
Seth, she'd take the prize for being foolish. Especially since they disagreed so strongly about
almost everything.

Seth had been going through the journal and
contemplating the different aspects of the map
ever since Melody had brought it to him on Friday.
While he did have a sense of exploration that had
been awakened, he hadn't been able to just give
himself over to the idea. He understood the mag-
nitude of the discovery of the map and the journal.
While the facts about the man were slim, her
documentation of his grandfather's infatuation
with the finding of the treasure was unbelievably
poignant. He wasn't sure if her writing had any
real historical value, but as a link to understanding his ancestor, it was of great value. His grandfather had basically abandoned his family, leaving
Jane and his son, Mason, to handle the running of

the stagecoach house on their own. Oh, he was a regular at the town saloon and the gambling tables, but now Seth knew what he did during the day. It was ridiculous. Unconscionable. And after reading the journal, he was all the more convinced no one would ever find the treasure if it existed. If Oakley had spent years pursuing the treasure, how did Melody think they would be doing anything but wasting their time? After all, his grandpa wasted his life…and missed out on his family's life, too.

But even knowing this with his practical brain all it took was one look at the hurt and anger he glimpsed in Melody's eyes for his impractical brain to make an aggressive attack on him.

He was standing at the back of the church auditorium when she entered the side door. The women rotated in and out of nursery duty and hers must have just been for the Sunday school hour. He watched her scan the room, hesitate when she saw him and then take the seat. He'd never before thought that she purposefully chose her seat according to where he was sitting…after all, they'd hardly known each other before she moved into the stagecoach house. But today, he knew without a doubt that he was exactly the reason she chose her seat. And that was exactly the reason he excused himself from his conversation and made his way across the room, up the far, outer aisle and slipped into the seat directly behind her.

Leaning forward, close to her ear, he murmured, "Still mad at me?" The soft scent drew him closer than necessary so when she turned sharply to look at him their faces were a mere inch apart. She leaned away to meet his gaze more fully.

"Yes."

It was so matter-of-fact that it startled a chuckle from him. He'd half expected her to deny it when he knew just by looking at her that she was fuming inside. And hurt…and that was what bothered him. She was too gentle, too easily victimized and he didn't like the idea that holding back on something she wanted so badly hurt her. The choir had started singing, and everyone was standing to sing the first song. He realized he and Melody were staring at each other and still sitting. She realized it, too. Jerking to a standing position, she grabbed a songbook and began furiously flipping pages. He stood more slowly, plucked a hymnal from the back of the pew and flipped through it as he contemplated his next move. The song was almost over when he realized he was holding his songbook upside down.

\* \* \*

The man was haunt—no he was *taunt*ing her, Melody thought an hour after she left church. Settling on the floor amid a stack of computer printouts on money stolen and attributed to Sam Bass and his gang, she vowed to kick Seth out of her head. Hours later as darkness fell, she kept coming back to Sam's biggest score. Coffee in hand, she carried the pages to the couch and curled up with a blanket, letting the stories roll through her head.

The outlaw, in her estimation, was more of a bungler than a skilled outlaw. The single documented robbery of a substantial amount was the sixty thousand dollars in gold pieces that he and his gang stole when they robbed the Union Pacific in Ogallala, Nebraska, in 1877…or, depending on which account she was looking at, it was documented to have taken place in Big Springs, Nebraska—the next stop over. It was the largest documented train robbery to date, but Melody was always struck by the fact that Sam couldn't get the safe open on the train. The man hopped on a train unprepared to get the safe open in the event that no one had the combination—why would you go to all that trouble without a backup plan? Inside that safe was *two hundred thousand* dollars, but

Sam didn't have a plan other than to get the porter to open it for him. And he hadn't been the good ole boy many gave him credit for being, because he pistol-whipped the poor man, trying to force him to tell the combination, which it turned out the porter didn't know.

Then, no safe to rob, one of Sam's gang members found some silver bullion in bricks but it was too *heavy* for them to carry…oh, yes, a greedy, stupid gang, to her mind.

It wasn't until one of the gang members found two small boxes sealed with sealing wax that they hit pay dirt. When they opened the boxes, they discovered the sixty thousand in gold coins. Luck, pure and simple! There was absolutely no skill involved. And that's why the line between legend and truth fascinated her. How could a loser like Sam Bass get such a mystic admiration built around him?

Especially since after the discovery of the coins they continued on and robbed the *passengers*. This netted a total of four hundred dollars. So there it was, if they hadn't happened upon the gold coins, this robbery would have yielded the gang a mere four hundred dollars and the only memorable part of the tale would have been the fact that the gang had been too unprepared for the job to steal the large money. Instead they'd gone down in history as the gang who'd, to date, pulled off the largest train heist ever. It was laughable; it was so crazy.

Melody was of the mind that Sam Bass was a legend that was stretched way out of proportion. Much of the money supposedly buried across Texas by him and his gang was probably pure legend. But there was the real mystery around what exactly happened to that sixty thousand dollars.

Once leaving the train, the men split the money and separated into pairs. A set of men was killed a week later, another set separated and one man was captured while it was rumored but not confirmed that the other escaped with his gold to Canada. The last two men, Sam Bass and Jack Davis, came back to Denton, Texas, and within four months were back robbing stagecoaches. What happened to all their money? Some stories were that they'd spent it on a life of extravagance. But ten thousand dollars each—that was an exorbitant amount of money in the 1870s and seemed too large to blow in such a short time period. So some believe they hid it in caves in the Hill Country…and this was only one of a massive amount of documented tales. And it did nothing to help her figure out who was supposed to have been on Seth's property. These two men didn't die here in the stagecoach house. In 1878, Sam was shot during a bank robbery and died in Round Rock, Texas, and *The Ballad of Sam Bass* was written soon after and became a song sang by cowboys for years to soothe restless cattle—go figure. Davis, though, seemingly disappeared, though some said he went to New Orleans.

Unless…Melody sucked in a sharp breath as an idea came to her. It was logical. Doable.

Jumping from the couch she did a little happy dance. She may have just figured out the map's creator.

## Chapter Nine

Melody prayed for courage. She felt like the lion in *The Wizard of Oz* as she drove toward Seth's the next morning. It had taken all her self-discipline not to hop in her car and rush over here last night. Still, in the bright light of day, she was full of hope that today he would listen to her. And she was going to have to get back the courage she'd had when she'd told him she wasn't giving up her lease on the stagecoach house. She needed that rebellious gal to show up and stand up for what was right.

Driving over his cattle guard, her adrenaline was pumping and inside she felt that burning excitement. He was pulling away from his barn in his truck pulling a horse trailer behind him.

Heart pumping, she slammed on her brake and

bounded out of her car. He halted too, but before he could get out she was at his open window.

"I think I know who our man is. The one who wrote the map."

"Are you all right?"

"No. I'm not. Didn't you hear me? I'm almost certain—well not certain but have an idea that our man is one of two people. He might have been Canadian Tom Nixon from Sam Bass's gang. Or Jack Davis."

Seth had gotten out of the truck as she talked and was grinning at her. "I had a feeling you were poring through your research yesterday. So what makes you think this?" He leaned a hip against his truck and crossed his boots at the ankle, doing the same with his arms across his chest. He looked so relaxed and in tune to what she had to say that Melody's mind went blank looking at him. Goodness, but the man had a way of throwing her off-kilter.

Taking a deep breath, she regrouped and told him about the story she'd kept going back to and how it had finally dawned on her. "You see, here it is, and it's a big what-if, because it would mean Tom Nixon didn't do what everyone thought he did. See, after the gang robbed the train they split the twenty-dollar gold pieces up between them, then split up into twos. The one couple was soon killed and Bass and Davis went back to Texas. The third couple, Nixon and Berry, ended up in Missouri, where Berry flaunted his money and was captured. And that's where it gets blurry. History says that Nixon then made his way back to Canada and then vanished, never to be heard from again." She was so excited relating her story to Seth that she was talking with her hands and firing out the tale with lightning speed. It was a wonder he could keep up with her but she couldn't help herself. When she came to a halt, practically gasping to get a breath, she realized he was looking at her in a way that made her insides melt. She swallowed hard and lost her train of thought again.

"Go on. I'm all ears," he urged.

"G-good," she managed. "Because this is important."

"I can see that."

"Good. H-here's what I think. What if Nixon didn't go from Missouri to Canada, but instead headed back to Texas with plans to join up with Bass and Davis again? But he ended up here in your ravine, got sick and your ancestors found him. What if that treasure map is to his share of the train robbery? If that's the case, then that's why none of this shows up in any record. He wasn't supposed to be in Texas. Or Davis, who also disappeared into history, at least from what I can find out so far, might also have been our man."

There, she'd finished. She stood, arms akimbo, and looked triumphantly at Seth. Sure this might not have been Nixon or Davis and sure there were tons of other possibilities. But this was plausible, and it was a good reason to convince Seth to pursue the treasure. "See, we have to go look for this treasure. You can't just ignore all of this. I won't let you, buster."

He laughed then. It was a sudden, unexpected hoot of laughter that was accompanied by twinkling eyes that seemed to reach out and grab her.

"Do you have any idea how cute you are when you're excited like this? No, of course you don't."

She'd thought through many things he might say to her after her disclosure, and she'd come up with counters to defend her position. Those words hadn't ever been in the running. She just blinked and felt ridiculously thrilled.

"Okay," he said, pushing away from the truck. "Come on."

Her brow crinkled, and her brain started working again. "What did you say?"

He grinned. "I said come on. I was on my way to your house when you drove up. I've got the horses loaded and thought today would be a great day for a treasure hunt."

Her mouth fell open in shock. He lifted his hand and placed his fingers beneath her chin, gently lifting up, so that her lips came together. "There ya go. Want to get this show on the road?"

Melody went from being the lion in *The Wizard of Oz* to Alice falling through the rabbit hole. "Y-you were coming to get me?"

He nodded, giving her a mischievous look—it was a new look for him and it kicked her pulse into high gear. Or maybe it was just the fact that this combined with knowing she stood up for what she believed in again was doing a number on her. Or maybe it was simply that she could feel the tingle of his touch all the way to the tips of her toes—even though his fingers were now curled around his truck's door handle.

He chuckled and said gently, "Well, do you want to do this or what?"

Melody wasted no time cutting her engine and scrambling inside Seth's truck. No way was she giving him time to change his mind.

"Do you ride?" he asked as the truck bumped across the pastures toward the ravine.

Talk coherently, she urged herself. "No, but I'd love to learn." It was the truth. "Is that possible?"

He cocked his head her way while a slow smile spread like a soft breeze across his face, filling his eyes with a dangerous light. "Oh, yeah, it's possible. But maybe today you'll just ride with me?"

She was *so* down the rabbit hole. There was no mistaking that the man was flirting with her! A thrill raced through her at the unlikely notion suddenly come true.

They'd reached the ravine, and he halted the truck and switched off the key. "You ready to go find a treasure?" he asked. She nodded. "Good, let's roll." He opened his door and was out before she could find her voice.

After unloading the horse from the trailer, he swung into the saddle, then helped her up behind him. She was treading on territory she'd never trodden before, and she felt shaky and more unsure of herself than ever. But either he didn't seem to notice or she was hiding her nerves better than she thought.

"So, why did you change your mind?" she asked as they rode on horseback through the trees. Somewhere in the few minutes it took him to unload the sand-colored horse and pull her up behind him in the saddle she'd decided her last course of action was to realize that Seth was probably just trying to ease the tension that had been between them. With that revelation, she was able to keep her head out of the clouds and concentrate on what had gotten them here…treasure.

"My brother reminded me that—" Seth started to say, glancing over his shoulder, enjoying the feel of her arms around his waist. The reality was that he'd struggled with himself all Sunday afternoon. After seeing Melody at church and listening to a message that had him wondering if Pastor Allen had been peeking into his head. The message was that God gave us opportunities to be blessings and to be blessed, but we needed to be ready to accept and act upon those opportunities. Seth couldn't deny that he was attracted to Melody. He also couldn't deny that despite all the treasure talk his thoughts inevitably went back to finding her crying that morning after the phone call. He didn't want gold diggers on his property, but he wanted to be around Melody and he wanted to help her if he could. All of the above had ultimately changed his mind but he wasn't about to tell Melody that. So instead he only said, "I remembered that I used to enjoy this sort of thing."

"Really?"

He did a double take of her expression. It alone said she couldn't imagine such a thing. Had he become that much of a stuffed shirt like his brothers kept telling him? "Why does that shock you so much?"

"I just can't picture you running around out here—" She stopped and turned a tinge of pink.

They were heading downhill and he watched ahead of them.

"I didn't mean that as an insult," she added.

"Oh, yeah right. You've been asking me to loosen up ever since you moved in out here." Her arms tightened around him momentarily as she stretched forward to look up at him.

"I have not—"

"Have, too," he cut in, grinning. "Me. Here. That's me loosening up, wouldn't you say?"

"Yes, you're right. And thank you," she agreed just as Dough Boy, Seth's horse, started down an incline and her arms tightened about him.

"That's it, hold on tight," he urged. "This might get tricky." And he wasn't just talking about the horse ride.

"You don't have to tell me twice," Melody said.

A few minutes later he held her hand as she slid to the ground and then he followed. They made their way down to the rocks he'd shown her before.

"So this is where we start," she said. "These do look pretty much like matching rocks. And this is the south end of the ravine?" Hands on hips, she intently surveyed the rocks.

Seth could see the excitement in her expression. "Roger that on both counts," he said. "If we follow the instructions, it would be fifty steps west."

She pointed east and looked at him. "Right?"

He grinned. "Actually," he leaned around her and pointed in the opposite direction. "It's that way. The woods have you turned around."

She bit her lip and got a crinkle between her brows. "I'd love to give the woods credit for my lack of direction but sadly I can't. I'm directionally challenged."

"Then remind me not to let you go running around out here alone."

"Oh, believe me, if I got lost out here, I'd find a rock to sit on and I'd wait for you to bring the posse looking for me."

She smiled up at him. "Good, that's exactly what I'd hope you would do. It's the smart move."

"The smart move will be for me to stick with you," she said.

"Now you're talking." They held gazes for a heartbeat.

"Th-then let's get going," she said and started walking. She hadn't taken two steps when she paused. "Do you think he meant regular steps or small, heel-to-toe steps? I *think* he would mean regular steps." She arched a brow in question.

"I agree...but when you get to about midway, we'll start looking for anything that might look promising."

"Right." She resumed walking and counting. He trailed behind, content to watch her throw herself into the hunt. With each step she counted, the excitement in her voice built.

"Twenty-five," she sang and came to a halt. "Do you see anything around here that looks like a tower?"

Seth scanned the area. "Not that I can tell. Keep going."

She started counting again immediately. The way had grown increasingly dense as they went. She had to push through underbrush and duck under tree limbs. Seth glanced back at the rocks to make sure they were holding their course. They were, he thought.

"Fifty." Melody glanced over her shoulder. "What do you think?"

They were standing in an overgrown area. Pines towered above them, almost blocking all the sunlight. "I hate to tell you, but I don't see anything that resembles a tower."

She frowned. "I know. So now what?" Disappointment rang in her voice as she scanned the area.

"I've been trying to figure out what he could have meant by towers, and I've come up blank."

"Maybe it's just something that we'll understand when we see it."

"Maybe so."

"Do you think there were pines here all those years ago?"

"Probably," he said. "Let's go this way and get out of the trees some." Seth led the way. But he knew he was only humoring Melody. He knew there wasn't anything in this area that was a tower. He just didn't have the heart to tell her she was on a wild-goose chase.

## Chapter Ten

"Well, what do ya know?" Sam said as Melody slid into the seat across from Seth. "How are ya?"

She plucked the menu from its sitting place between the napkin holder and the bottle of hot sauce, feeling uneasy. They'd been driving back to her house when Seth said he was heading into town to grab a burger. He'd suggested that since it was so late she might want to join him. She kept reminding herself that his asking was simply because it was the polite thing for him to do. She could have refused, given him the easy out, but she hadn't.

Something told her that her phone at home was probably ringing, and she just couldn't face that notion tonight.

"I'm fine, Mr. Greene," she said. "How are you?"

"Now, hold on a minute. How many times do I have to tell you to call me Sam? My daddy was Mr. Greene, and he didn't much care for the formality of it either."

"Yes, sir—Sam."

"Now that's more like it. Ain't nothin' in this town formal, most especially this joint with all these ugly ole cowboys." A big hoot rang out from the roomful of cowboys and brought a good-natured scowl from Sam. "Not only are they ugly but they've got big ears. And this ugly thang your with ain't much better—"

"Hey," Seth protested with a grin. "You're supposed to be nice to your customers, not harass them."

"I am bein' nice—to the one who counts."

Melody smiled. Sam loved to give the cowboys a hard time. But he was always sweet to the women. Most of the women, that was—he did like to tease Norma Sue and Esther Mae. "I'll bet you'll be glad when Miss Adela gets home," she said quietly.

He beamed. "Tomorrow can't get here soon enough! I know my Adela and Norma Sue and Esther Mae had a good time, but I don't know if I could make it another day without seein' her beautiful smile."

"I'm sure she's just as anxious to see you, too," Melody said.

Seth raised a brow. "Obviously, all we ugly cowboys will be glad for her to get home too, so he'll stop mistreating us."

That brought on a wave of grunted agreements, and when Melody met Seth's gaze, he winked at her. It was pretty pathetic that a wink could send her world spinning, but it did. In all her life not once had it ever happened before.

Seth cupped his hands together on the table and leaned forward after Sam left with their order. "So, tell me what you like most about teaching."

Her heart warmed to him even more at the question. "I love the kids."

"Why?"

That threw her a little. "Why not? They're great."

He shook his head. "Too easy. I'm digging for info here, and you're hording it. Why do you love to teach?"

A small laugh escaped her. He really wanted to know her better. It was a breathtaking thought. "Fourth graders are my favorite age. Because, see, they're really settling into their personalities. They're finding out who they are and exploring that. While at the same time, they are very open to influence. And they are just so funny, so full of life." In the background, someone had put a quarter in the jukebox and Vince Gill's beautiful voice gently filled the room.

"And you, the quiet teacher, likes them to be full of life?"

"I love it! I encourage it."

He was taking a drink of his tea and choked at her answer. "Like how?" he coughed, his eyes dancing over the top of the fist he'd lifted to his lips.

"Well, like this one little girl who was so shy at the beginning of the year that she wouldn't ask questions. She sat beside the cutest little blond. He had a rep from the year before as being the class clown. And it was so true. This boy just couldn't stop himself from entertaining once he realized he had an audience. The kid would just get louder and louder, and I'd have to ask him to quiet down. It was very disruptive so I had to start giving him assignments to help me do things. By the end of the year he'd become a leader in the best sense of the word."

"Really?"

"Well, no," she confessed. "But, he had *moments* when he shined and he took his tasks seriously. And he did them with a smile. He will be a leader, it's obvious. But the best part was he actually countered the girl's quieter side."

"Yours, too."

She gave him a teasing smile. "Yes, but don't tell anyone."

"I wouldn't think of it."

"Good." She propped her elbow on the table and cupped her chin as she looked at him. "I absolutely loved that kid for bringing the little girl out of her shell—which he worked at."

He really liked her. "I can see why you would."

"Yes, but I love the teaching, too. I mean, you know me, how I get when I'm talking about history."

"I like it when you talk about history."

"You do?"

"I can't imagine anyone not enjoying *you* talking about anything."

Melody's heart started drumming. She could talk to him without feeling self-conscious. She wondered if he even knew that he made her feel pretty with the intense way he held her gaze with his. Or with the flirting—or teasing that he was doing.

She wondered if he had any idea how alive she felt sitting across from him.

When Sam finally brought out their food, it was a given that Melody had never had a better burger and fries in all of her life. Their meal had taken a rather long time to get to them—not that she minded. She enjoyed talking to Seth, and it was nice to think that Seth had enjoyed talking to her.

\* \* \*

"I had a good time today," she said as they drove up in front of her house. The night was bright. Moonlight bathed everything in a silver shadow, and Melody felt breathless with the romance of it all. Not that this was really romance. But a girl could dream.

"I did, too," he said, softly turning to look at her, resting his right arm across the back of the seat.

Melody was so aware of how close his fingertips were to her shoulder. It was silly, but she yearned with every fiber of her being that he would touch her. And yet she knew wishing such a thing was dangerous. The baggage she carried into a relationship…it was too much. What man would want a woman who had the troubles that clung to her because of Ty? "I have to go," she said, fumbling for the door handle. She was certain he could hear the pounding of her heart, she was in such a panic. The door opened at last, just as he'd started to reach across her to open it. She almost fell out of the truck trying to get away.

"I'll pick you up in the morning?"

She nodded.

"Then it's a date."

She wished.

She nodded. "Thanks for a lovely day," she

managed to say. "See you in the morning." And then she ran…well, she walked, but mentally she was running. When she reached the porch, she dared to turn and watch him drive away on the silver ribbon of road that glistened like a moonbeam.

She told herself she was on dangerous ground. If she woke tomorrow to realize none of the day had really happened she wouldn't be surprised at all. She knew it was too beautiful to be anything but a dream. She'd been right to come to her senses and remember that she had Ty and his addictions hanging around her neck like a dead weight.

And as if she needed any proof of what her reality was, she found it as soon as she opened her door and saw the blinking red light on her answering machine.

"You ready for some adventure?" Seth asked the next morning as Melody tugged open the door. But one look at her and he knew something was wrong. He'd found himself fascinated by her the day before. He'd been champing at the bit for the morning to come so he could see her again. Last night he'd intentionally steered the conversation toward finding out more about her. And he'd liked her all the more. Two weeks ago he couldn't begin to picture her controlling a class of rambunctious fourth graders. He'd figured they'd run all over her, but now, having seen her spunk shining through on several occasions, he knew that she might struggle every once in a while, but from the stories she told as a whole, her class didn't push her too hard. For that, he also found himself saying a prayer of thanks to the Lord…obviously He'd gone easy on her by giving her students who wanted to learn. Of course, once she started talking it was pretty hard to look away from her, and he could see her having the exact same effect on her class. She was infectious in a wonderful way.

Today he wanted to learn everything he could about her. And he wanted to start by finding out why her eyes looked haunted today instead of excited. He had a feeling he knew.

"Sorry," she said. "I'm running a bit late. The— a phone call held me up."

He'd known it before she confirmed his suspicions. "Do you mind if I grab myself a cup of that coffee I smell?" he asked, following her into the hall.

She looked nervous standing there with her bare feet peeking from beneath her jeans as she fingered her socks. "I just need to get my boots on and then we can run—get out of here."

He strolled into the kitchen with her following him. "No need to hurry," he said, fully suspecting that her words hadn't just gotten mixed up. She was ready to bolt as quick as she could, and he wanted to know why someone on the other end of a phone had the power to make her want to run. "You put your boots on, and I'll pour my own coffee."

She hesitated as if contemplating telling him that they didn't have time for him to drink a cup of coffee. He reached for a cup from the drain board, and she sank into a chair at the table and started to pull on her socks. He tried to choose the right approach as he poured his coffee, then leaned a hip against the counter and watched her. Seeing her fumble to get the socks in place sent that out the window. "Is something bothering you?" he asked frankly.

Her head shot up. "No."

"You really aren't going to sit there and tell me that when anyone with half a brain can see something is bothering you." A bit harsh but he suddenly wasn't feeling real touchy-feely. He wanted to know what was causing that look in her eyes.

She yanked her second sock on and stood up just as the phone rang.

"I'll get that," he said, reacting to the fact that she'd jumped at the sound. He didn't know what was going on but it was about to stop—

"No!" she exclaimed, shooting past him to

snatch the cordless phone from the counter. "I'll get it," she said, and strode past him into the hall.

He watched her go, heard her hesitant hello as he stalked to the kitchen door. He had to plant his feet in order not to follow her and take the phone back from her. There was no rain to shield her words, and because she hadn't closed her door all the way, her words drifted easily to him.

"Ty, don't start. N-no, I'm sorry you don't have any money…I wasn't ignoring you…take it easy. No, this isn't my fault…"

Seth's fist curled around the door frame.

"I—I can't keep living like this—" she said, and he heard weariness in her voice. "All right, all right. I'll call the bank tomorrow and transfer the money."

*"What?"* Seth growled, strode down the hall and pushed open her door.

"I have to go," she said quickly and clicked the disconnect button. "What are you doing?" she asked as he took the phone from her.

"You might be surprised to know I'm not a man who'll stand by and see some jerk mistreat a woman. Is this Ty your boyfriend?"

"You had no business listening to my conversation," she snapped, brushing past him and stalking down the hallway.

"Wait, you're mad at *me?*" he asked, following

her back into the kitchen, totally baffled by her. "You're as white as a sheet, and you're shaking, too." He yanked a chair out from the table, grabbed her by the shoulders and gently guided her to sit. He stooped down in front of her. She wouldn't look at him.

"I'm not mad, I just—let's just go treasure hunting."

"Forget it. You're upset. Look, if the guy is mistreating you then tell me. I'll put a stop to it." Seth hadn't been this mad in a long time.

"You don't understand. It's not like that. Ty is my brother."

That set him back on his heels. "Your *brother?*" He stared at her as she nodded. Seth didn't think he'd ever seen anything as sad as the look in her eyes. "Why would your brother treat you this way?"

Her lip trembled and a tear rolled down her cheek. She brushed it away and looked away from him. Unable to help himself, he touched his hand to the side of her face, gently turning it back to him. "Talk to me," he urged gently. "It looks to me like you could use someone in your corner." It was hard for her. Her eyes said so, but Seth thought he saw a glimmer of want in there. She looked away, not ready. He'd only heard her side of the conversation, but that was enough for him to know that he would have hurt Ty if he could have gotten to him.

Now he wanted to wrap her in his arms and comfort her. He stood instead. "I tell you what. Let's get out of here. A ride on a horse and some fresh air will do you some good. Might even prove to you that you can trust me." That won him a small smile. "How does that sound?"

"That sounds good. Thank you."

"You might not thank me later. We're going to continue this conversation soon—you have my word on that," he warned as he tugged her out of the chair and gave her a hug. She needed it—at least that's what he told himself as he wrapped his arms around her. She was tense but melted against him for a second, taking comfort and, he hoped, his strength. He'd glimpsed the whisper of a stronger woman over the last few days. The woman who'd stood up to him and refused to leave the coach house was inside Melody, only that woman wasn't home at the moment. He was overwhelmingly protective of the one who was.

She pulled away almost the instant she'd relaxed against him, and reluctantly he let her go. The idea that she didn't stay in his arms could be interpreted several ways. One, she didn't like being hugged by him. Or two, she didn't like giving in to her weakness…he liked the second interpretation better. For both their sakes.

## Chapter Eleven

Melody was feeling better. Riding on a horse with her arms around Seth was the ultimate distraction from her problems. He hadn't pressured her to talk as they'd ridden. The fact that he'd placed his free hand over hers had startled her when he'd done it. She told herself it was simply him giving her reassurance…which in and of itself was a revelation she couldn't totally get used to.

But he'd wanted to stand up for her. And in her kitchen when he'd taken such gentle care of her, settling her into a chair when her knees had almost given way…it had been so sweet. And of course the hug.

And he was asking her to trust him. One look into his eyes as he'd knelt there in front of her and she'd wanted to spill her guts to him. She'd wanted to ask him what he would do in her situation and pray that in doing so everything would be made right.

It had been a daydream in the midst of her breakdown. It was beautiful and calming to remember that moment. But this was a private matter. Hadn't her parents taught her that some things needed to remain in the family?

They'd dismounted and were about to go in on foot. He hadn't asked questions as they'd ridden, giving her time to think. "Ty is a drug-addict— drug and alcohol." She blurted the confession out before she could second-guess herself. It was surprisingly freeing to say the words.

"Him and half the world it seems sometimes," he said. "Why does he call you?"

Melody thought about changing the subject but she'd already opened the dam and the idea of verbalizing the problem was...needed.

"He can't hold down a job. I pay his rent and utilities."

"Why do you do that?"

*Why?* "Because he needs me."

"But he's a man, right? A *grown* man?"

"Yes, but this has been going on for a long time. And I don't know what to do for him. My parents were killed in a car wreck a few years ago, and I've basically taken over doing what they were doing."

"And that's paying his bills."

"Yes. He's been in and out of rehab but nothing has worked. He always goes back to using. But I can't afford to pay for his rehab so if he goes in now it's to a state-funded program. I'm trying to get him to get help and I thought, maybe if I didn't give him money, he would go. But the places aren't that great—"

"As in not plush."

"Well, yes. They're pretty bare bones."

"But they do the job."

"I guess. If he would go." But it looked like that wasn't going to happen.

"If he won't go that shouldn't be your problem. He's a big boy."

There was no sympathy in Seth's words. "I know." She sighed. "I moved here trying to distance myself from him. Hoping that would help me be able to make hard choices, but it hasn't helped. He keeps promising me he's going to check in to one of those rehabs, but he hasn't. So I thought I'd try and be hard-nosed…cut him off and give him the ultimatum that he has to help himself."

"Which is the right outlook. He's a grown man.

And he's using you. Not to mention abusing you and you're letting him. That's not good, Melody."

"Yes, that's what I've come to realize. I didn't realize how badly my parents had gone into debt paying for the rehab and paying his expenses all those years. I can't let him do that to me."

"Good for you."

"No, it's not that easy. That's what I keep thinking but when he calls, he's so desperate. I always give in." Like she'd just agreed to do again.

"When he calls and chews you out?"

She nodded. She could feel her cheeks warm with embarrassment. She sounded like a pushover.

"You're right. You need to cut the purse strings."

Melody looked away. She was trying to cut the purse strings but it wasn't as easy as it sounded. "I'll do it next month."

"You need to stick to your decision this time and not send him the money you told him you'd send earlier."

Melody crossed her arms and stared down the steep incline to the place where they would begin the hunt for the treasure. "Are we going to try and figure out the map?"

"In a minute. Are you going to send him the money? He's using you."

She spun toward him. "I already told him I'd send it."

"That's not helping him. And it certainly isn't helping you."

His words cut across her heart like only the truth can do. But still, the sound of desperation hadn't been missed in Ty's voice. As it always did, it conjured up images for her of him walking the streets—living on the streets. And it also brought the promise she'd made her mother crashing down on her shoulders. "Seth, at the hospital just before my mother died she begged me to take care of him. How can I go against that and put Ty out on the street? If he would just agree to go into rehab—"

Seth scowled. "Obviously that's not going to happen. Let him fall on his face. It's the only way. It's hard to think about, but, sadly, at this point it's the right thing to do."

"What about the Christian thing to do? Ty calls me a hypocrite every other breath."

"He's playing you. Christians aren't supposed to fall down and let people walk over the top of them. Sure you're supposed to turn the other cheek, to an extent. But there is a line that has to be drawn. He isn't good for you."

"You hardly know me—"

"I think I know you better than you think. I've

watched you for two years since you came here, and you're like a shadow. You don't get involved much and I thought it was because you were shy…but you aren't shy. You're hiding. I've seen it in the last week since I've gotten to know you better. You actually have some guts. And I think if you got this monkey off your back and actually lived your life, instead of the life your brother is dictating for you, that you'd be the outgoing person you're supposed to be."

Anger spiked through her like a fever. She'd thought telling him would help relieve some of the pressure she was feeling. Instead he was adding pressure to her. She inhaled sharply and tried to hold her tongue. It was true that she was withdrawn a lot of the time because she just had things on her mind and, well, she was shy. "I'm quiet, naturally."

"You're repressed." His look almost dared her to disagree.

She glared at him. "*Repressed?* As in reserved, yes I am. That's easy enough to see. You say it like it's a dirty word."

"Not dirty. Just hiding. You're repressed as in you suppress painful things and withdraw inside because of them. How much of your childhood was overshadowed because of the attention given to Ty's destructive lifestyle?"

*Most of it.* She stiffened, thinking of how his problems had always taken the joy out of almost everything. Like so many other times growing up, her parents' devotion to helping Ty or getting him out of trouble always trumped other things. They forgot several of her birthdays because they were dealing with Ty issues. They even missed her college graduation because they had to take Ty to yet another rehab. But it had been important…feeling resentment about such things seemed mean and selfish. She'd never let anyone know that it bothered her. Seth was right, though; she had withdrawn and held in her feelings. And she felt guilty for having them. That Seth saw this in her made her feel exposed.

"Can we drop this? Please. I want to get down there and see if this is the place."

"Why, so you can pretend it's not the truth? So you can go on hiding from the facts?"

"Back off, Seth." She exploded. "How's that? Get off my back, all right."

"Mad is good," he said.

Melody started down the hill—it was either that or she might haul off and hit him! She'd never hit anyone in her life. It was a horrible thing to think. And the idea that she was so mad at him scared her.

* * *

What was he doing? Seth watched Melody tromp down the hill. She was already stressed out of her mind and he was sticking his nose where it didn't belong. This was not like him at all, and he knew it was because he had feelings for Melody.

There was just no denying the fact. But that didn't give him the right to step over boundaries...especially since he was such a strong believer that people should honor them.

Melody was giving off *more* than just a hint that she didn't want to talk about her brother. It was evident that criticizing the way she was handling her brother was not a way to endear himself to her. And he wanted her to like him. He wanted to test the waters and see if there was a future between them. He knew that he'd never had this strong a connection with any other woman.

*But she needed to hear the truth.* And she needed not to let this jerk run over her any more. And he needed to back off.

For now anyway. Not so she would like him but so she could calm down and listen to reason.

Melody was halfway to the rocks when she heard Seth behind her. She was breathing hard from hurrying and it was a wonder she hadn't tripped and broken her neck—as if the thought was all it took her toe to hit a snag.

Seth's hand on her arm gave her just the balance she needed. "Steady there," he said, moving beside her. "Look, I'm sorry. I overstepped my bounds."

She didn't look at him but slowed her pace. "I want to hunt for the treasure. I—" she looked at him then "—I don't want to think about Ty. Is that so wrong?"

He looked like there was so much he wanted to say. She braced herself for it. "No," he said, taking the lead. "I came to hunt for treasure, too, so let's get to it."

The tension between them was there; it wasn't something she could escape. He'd said he was sorry but not that he was wrong. He thought she was weak, repressed and hiding…not a very good boost to her already low opinion of herself. She trudged behind him and drove her thoughts forward to the map and what could be waiting for them if they could just focus.

They hiked all the way down the ravine to the river's edge and nothing looked remotely like towers. Melody had known better than to get her hopes up. What would the odds have been that she would find the treasure on the first or second exploration?

"Now what?" she said, scanning the river. It was moving slowly at this point, and there was a rope hanging from a tree. She pictured Seth as a teen swinging from the rope and dropping into the water.

"Well, this is a big place. I'm not convinced the man would have known the west end from the south end once he was in here."

Melody turned to look back up the grueling climb they'd made down to the river. Then she turned in rotation, taking in all the vegetation. "I personally couldn't have done it. But that's me. You could have."

"Yeah, but I've roamed these woods all my life. Wyatt and Cole couldn't do it. They could come close but only because of the time they spent here with me leading the way."

"I didn't realize when I found the map that the real mystery was simply going to be figuring out the beginning point. And that would mean figuring out what made the man tick."

Seth pushed his hat back. "Come on, let's keep looking." He led the way beside the river but hadn't gone far when the sky started to darken and the wind started to pick up. He studied the sky. "Not good. It looks like rain." He halted, not looking happy. "The weather man predicted forty-percent chance. That looks a little more like a sure thing than I'm comfortable with." He looked apologetically at her. "Sorry, but I think we'd better head back."

"But—" She started to protest just as a big rain drop plopped between her eyes.

"Yep. Come on," he said. He had no more spoken the words when the sky opened up and a torrential downpour came raining down on them.

Texas weather! They were soaked instantly.

"This way," Seth shouted over the onslaught. "We need to climb back up the ravine before too much of this rain falls or else we're going to get stuck having to walk out from down here."

"Why is that bad?" she asked, trying to keep up with him as he backtracked along the river.

"It's an all-day walk to follow the river out." Rain was dripping off his hat and running down the back of his neck as he indicated the way they'd come through the trees. He started up then turned to reach for her hand. She blinked through the curtain of water falling off of her bangs and straight into her eyes as she took his hand.

She immediately felt security in his strong grip. Already the black clay that marbled the terrain was turning to slick slip-and-slides. Her boots slid as he tugged her forward through the pine and oak trees. It was tough going, and she was gasping through the water and the sticky humid air that covered them. In no time at all she was sweating despite the rain. All the way, Seth kept a firm grip on her hand, practically pulling her along behind him. The steep incline hadn't been easy coming down in the best of conditions, but this was ridiculous!

Her boot hit a slick spot, and she went down on one knee. Her knee struck a rock hard. She bit back a cry of pain.

Seth's grip tightened as he spun toward her. "Are you okay? Your pant leg is ripped—"

"I'm fine," she called, speaking over the wind. "Go."

He nodded and continued on. "Sorry to pull you along so fast, but this is not the place to be when rains this heavy are coming down."

*No joke.* Rivers of water were coursing down now. Her boots were sticking in the clay and water swirled around her feet as it rushed downward. They still had a good thirty feet to go, but it was the steepest, roughest part of the incline, and looking at it, Melody's heart pounded with adrenaline and dread. If Seth wasn't holding her hand so tightly, there was no way she would be strong enough to fight the water and the slippery slope.

As if hearing her thoughts, he paused using a pine tree for balance and pulled her up into the shelter of his body. "We're not going to make it," he said close to her ear. "C'mon. This way." He started moving across the hill.

"Where are we going?" she called, grasping his hand with both of hers as he plowed forward. Even his sure-footed steps wobbled in the mud a time or two but he was able to keep himself from going down. She, on the other hand, went down several more times, and each time he pulled her up and pushed forward.

"There," he said.

Melody saw a rock ledge in front of them with water pouring over the top of it like a waterfall. She wasn't sure what he'd been thinking bringing them this way. But he kept heading toward the water rather than away. When they were ten feet from it, he turned to look at her.

"We're going under that ledge. It's a rock surface behind there, and it'll be somewhat dry."

Shivering, she nodded, game if he was. At the rock, he ducked down and pulled her through the side, which had a small veil of water compared to the mass that was churning over the front of the ledge.

He was right about it being dry once they were

beneath the rock. Seth crouched down, then sat because there wasn't any standing room. She did the same. Only then did she take a deep breath.

"That was crazy!" she exclaimed, wiping her face with her hands. Seth took his hat off and shook it then wiped his own face, swept his hair back off his forehead and replaced his hat. His expression was dark in the shadows of the rock.

"It was stupid on my part. I knew there was a forty-percent chance of thundershowers. I should never have kept you out here so long."

She was breathing hard. "It's not your fault."

His scowl deepened. "Yeah. It is. We should have turned back an hour ago. Flash floods aren't anything to take lightly out here. You and I both know how deadly they can be."

He was really upset. "Yes, but you knew your way around. You knew to come here. I would have seen this waterfall and never thought that it would be shelter. Have you been here before?"

"Yes, once when me, Cole and Wyatt were camping at the canyon, we got caught out here. Wyatt knew about this place because he'd stumbled across it when he'd been looking for a lost calf earlier that summer. We spent four hours sitting under here."

"It sounds like it was a great adventure."

His scowl eased up. "It was, looking back. But at the time we were bored out of our minds."

She immediately imagined three teenage guys going stir-crazy. "What did y'all talk about?"

Seth gave her a look that was so boyishly cocky that she had to chuckle again.

"Oh, let's see, what do you think? Girls and treasure."

She lifted a brow. "Of course. What else would three teenage guys talk about?"

He grunted and watched the curtain of water pouring over the ledge in front of him. She was so curious about him that she could hardly stand it. And she suddenly knew right then and there that this was the only place she wanted to be. It felt as if she and he were the only two people in the entire world. Nothing else mattered or could intrude on the time. Silly.

Melody wrapped her arms about herself and rubbed the water from her arms. "I can't believe how slippery the slope got," she said, refocusing her thoughts.

"I know how treacherous it can get and just how quickly. I should never have chanced coming out here today."

The disgust in his voice rang through the dim light in the overhang. "Hey, are you forgetting that I'm an adult? And as an adult I can make choices for myself. This is not your fault, and I won't have you blaming yourself. Besides, nothing has happened to us except we're wet." She glanced down at her throbbing knee for the first time.

Seth's gaze moved to her ripped jeans. "You're bleeding."

# Chapter Twelve

"It's not bad," Melody protested, the minute she saw the blood on her fingertips. Compared to the throbbing, the blood was nothing.

"Let me have a look at that," Seth said, carefully pushing aside the torn material. "Did you hit a rock?"

"Yes," she said, watching as he pulled his shirttail from his jeans and ripped off the bottom and gently applied pressure to the small gash. She gasped.

"Sorry," he said looking at her with sympathetic eyes. "I hate that you were walking when it was bleeding like this."

"I didn't even realize it was bleeding until now. Oddly enough. I guess I was having a delayed reaction to the pain, too. But it's feeling better." And it was. Seth bent closer to her knee and lifted the cloth. She shivered at the tenderness of his actions.

"Are you cold?" he asked.

"Just a little. But I'm okay. Really, I can do that. It's really not that bad."

"I'll take care of it."

Her thoughts were spinning crazily. More so when he suddenly ripped a longer piece from his shirttail then tied the pieces around her knee so that it held the makeshift bandage in place. It was so sweet that it almost undid her.

She was relieved when he withdrew his touch, hoping that with the absence of it she would stop thinking about how totally attracted to him she was. It was a short-lived relief when he slid next to her and draped his arm across her shoulders.

"Is that better?"

She nodded numbly and gave him a smile. "This isn't exactly the way I thought treasure hunting would be."

He chuckled and gave her a gentle squeeze. "It has been eventful."

"But not in the right way," she sighed.

"Hey, a guy could take that as an insult. Here you are stranded with me like this and saying very unflattering things about me."

"I didn't mean it that way. I—" she faltered at

the twinkle in his eyes looking at her "—I'm liking this part of the search, actually." Had she really said that? He looked as surprised by it as she was. She'd meant every word, but to have voiced it… Well, that was an entirely new ball game for her.

"Listen to you. That's the spunky woman I like."

"I can't believe I said that."

He smoothed a rogue strand of hair from her forehead with his fingertips. "*I* can. Don't forget, I was there the day you told me you weren't leaving my property and practically waved your lease in my face."

"I did not," she gasped, elbowing him.

He chuckled and cocked a brow. "I beg to differ."

Melody's breath caught looking at Seth. His teasing eyes darkened suddenly, and she knew he was thinking about kissing her. She swallowed hard, and felt sick—it was a good sick but it was sick nonetheless. This wasn't happening to her. Handsome men didn't look twice at her. They didn't notice her. To have Seth suddenly showing her what she was missing…she looked away from him. It was too hard to bear thinking that soon he would snap out of this, this feel-sorry-for-the-bookworm mode and he'd walk away. Only she knew that if he kissed her he would walk away with her heart and she would be shattered.

Her lip trembled as she watched the water pouring over the ledge, and suddenly she felt trapped behind the illusion that this was real. "I think the rain is slowing," she said. She needed to get out of there.

He didn't say anything for a moment, and she could feel his gaze on her, but she couldn't look at him. If she did, she'd probably throw herself at him—which would be kind of hard since she was already practically in his embrace.

"Melody," his voice melted through the shadows harmonizing with the last sounds of rain and cascading water.

She shook her head and refused to turn back. She was fighting for her life here. Couldn't he see that?

His arm loosened and after a second slid away from her. Relief and regret washed over her.

"Why do you hide from that part of yourself?"

His soft words lingered on the air. "Why do you insist on trying to make me into something I'm not?"

"That's a lie, and you know it."

At his cutting words she glared at him. "How dare you. You don't know me, Seth Turner. You don't know me at all."

"I'm beginning to think it's the other way around."

"What does that mean?"

"I'm not so sure you know yourself. You've got all this spirit inside of you and yet you hide it. When you do let it out, it's more rebellious than anything because you keep it so bottled up…or maybe it has to do with your brother."

That did it. She scrambled across the tight space so that she was sitting across from him. She refused to have even his elbow touching her.

"Look at you. Mention this guy and you immediately tie up in knots."

"Not true."

"Why don't you use some of that against your brother and what he's doing to your life?"

Why was he doing this? She looked away. The last thing she wanted to do was argue about her lack of backbone where Ty was concerned. But at least she wasn't thinking about kissing Seth any longer. What a cop-out on her part. It was a new all-time low for her, hiding behind her problem with Ty to protect her childish heart.

"Do you think you're doing him any favors enabling him like this?"

"No," she snapped, angry at herself as much she was at him.

"Then what is it?"

She glared at him. "I—I try to be firm. You just don't understand."

"No. I think I understand completely. He works you until he wears you down. I can understand that. He sees what I've seen of you all this time. Up until you told me you weren't leaving the coach house the other day, I had no idea there was any kind of spunk in you. Imagine my surprise to find out that beneath that shy exterior there is a woman to be reckoned with."

She gave a harsh laugh. "Hardly. I only stood up to you because I just couldn't give up on something I cared so much about."

"Yeah, so I figured that out. So why don't you show your brother the same kind of heart and stop enabling him?"

Every ounce of oxygen seemed to evaporate. She had to struggle to draw in her next breath. "It's complicated."

She stared at the water and willed it to stop.

"Try me. I'm a smart guy. I bet I can get it."

The man was pushing like a freight train, and she just didn't get why he was doing it. "Because my mother begged me to help him. Her last words to me before she died was that I help him. It's hard thinking about going against her last wish."

He dropped his head back and stared at the ceiling. "That has to be rough on you," he said at last.

She nodded, blinking at the unexpected and unwanted threat of tears. She'd never told anyone that.

"You can't do it. You can't use that as an excuse," he said gently. "You mentioned before that your parents were in debt because of all the money they put out for his treatments. Is that what your mother was asking you to do to yourself? Surely you see that you can't do that. Is that why you at least tried to cut him off?"

She nodded, biting her lip when it started to tremble. "But I feel like I've given up on him." Guilt filled her. "No. The honest truth is that I don't just feel like I've given up on him but I *have*. Worse than that—after all the treatments he's been through and after all the prayers…I've given up that God is ever going to honor my and my parents' prayers." She swallowed the lump in her throat as anger filled in behind the guilt. Her parents had been faithful to pray for Ty's deliverance from the addictions that plagued him, and they hadn't lived to see that deliverance. Even though they believed God would come through for them. "I tell myself I have to let him suffer the consequences of his actions. That all the money spent on him before was a waste because he didn't want to get free of the addictions. I tell myself all kinds of things, but when it comes down to letting my brother go hungry on the street with no shelter…I just can't do it. With or without the promise I made to my mom."

"So you're going to give in and let him treat you like a doormat? You're going to let this be your life?"

"Don't you think I despise myself for weakening? I always come back to the realization that this is the way my life will always be and I should just get used to it."

He tensed, his jaw set. "That's plain depressing."

"Tell me about it."

"Then say enough is enough and stop letting your mother's bad judgment call and your brother dictate your life."

"I know you're right." She did. "But I just get so tired." She felt tired thinking about it now. "Can we talk about something different?" She looked away, knowing she was a coward, but it was easy for someone who hadn't lived with what she'd lived with to tell her how to handle the situation. This was her life, and it wasn't as black and white as it appeared to others.

The community center was crowded as Melody walked in. She was comfortable here with her friends because they accepted her quietness without pushing her to step out of her box. Well, most of the time. There had been a few times when they'd urged her to date, but nothing had come of it and so they'd backed off. That had been a relief because she'd seen Norma Sue, Esther Mae and Adela zero in on someone and things just seemed to happen. Melody actually loved watching their antics. The matchmakers were pushy sometimes and subtle other times. There wasn't a person in Mule Hollow who didn't know that the three ladies were devoted to keeping their beloved little town alive and well for decades to come, and marrying off the cowboys who worked this cattle-rich area was their surefire way of getting it done.

Esther Mae was greeting everyone at the door. Melody smiled the minute she saw her. Esther loved hats but usually only wore them to church on Sunday mornings. Tonight, however, over her bright red hair she wore a wide-rimmed straw hat with a toy parrot perched on the hatband. The four-inch-tall bird was blindingly colorful as was Esther Mae's dress. "So what do you think?" she asked, twirling around so that the gauzy material flowed around her in a sea of florescent red, green and yellow.

"I love it," Melody said in all honesty. Esther Mae was the most colorful person she'd ever known, and the outfit matched her personality to perfection.

"I did, too. I have to say that I was the cat's meow on that ship."

"Cat's meow, my foot. You look like a hot air balloon!" Norma Sue barked. Marching over she engulfed Melody in a bear hug—which she was really good at, since she was an unapologetically robust woman. "You haven't gone off and married in the ten days we been gone, have you?"

"Now don't go and embarrass the girl," Esther Mae chided.

"You're telling *me* how not to embarrass a body!" Norma gave Melody an exasperated frown. "You should have seen the way people scattered when Esther Mae came flitting around on deck. And with good cause after she tripped over the hem of her muumuu and took out the entire dessert buffet—"

"Ha! It wasn't my muumuu but your *foot* I tripped over."

The room broke into chuckles as a mischievous grin spread across Norma Sue's face. Melody enjoyed their combative banter.

In contrast to her friends, Adela was dainty and

soft-spoken with short white hair that framed her face and caused her topaz eyes to sparkle like jewels. She came through the crowd and gave Melody a gentle but sincere hug. "Hello, dear. It is so good to see you," she said and then stepped back and gave her buddies a teasing look of reproach. "As all of you can tell, my dear friends had a wonderful time on the cruise. And they are both telling the truth in a manner of speaking. Yes, Esther Mae tripped over Norma Sue's foot and took out the dessert table. But in the process, they were such entertainment that the cruise line offered to hire them to come on other cruises as the secret entertainment."

Esther Mae jabbed a hand on her hip. "We would have been good, too. But a cruise ship just can't compare to Mule Hollow. Or my Hank."

"Amen to that," Norma Sue said. "We were ready to get home and get the Fourth of July celebration going. Lacy, hop on up there on that stage and tell us where we stand. We have as many out-of-town booth spaces rented out as last year?"

"We have a big turnout, Norma," Lacy called, springing onto the stage. Her shaggy blond hair danced as she swung toward the group. This was a big event for Mule Hollow. And it was always packed with vendors who had learned that when

Mule Hollow invited folks to come they came in droves. It was the first event Melody had attended when she got there. Though she hadn't been brave enough to do much, she had offered to work in the cotton candy booth. But even though she didn't toss a cow chip or race in the three-legged race or throw a ball at some poor cowboy in the dunking booth, it didn't mean she didn't enjoy herself. Because she did. It was great fun just watching everyone. Especially fun was when people climbed onto the mechanical bull. True, she had secretly wondered if it was as hard to stay on the bull as it looked. But to actually get out there and hop on that thing…oh, no, she would remain safely in the cotton candy booth.

She'd had a great view of the excitement last year when the Dog on a Stick vendor and the Taco Dude got into a fight over the affections of the Birdhouse lady or something like that. All the excitement had happened right in front of her booth, and poor Sheriff Brady had his hands full putting a stop to that fiasco. Melody figured if there was half the excitement this year she'd at least get a good laugh.

Except, she realized with a sense of foreboding that Lacy had changed her job this year.

Lacy wanted her out of the booth—out in the

open. That right there should scare the daylights out of her. But it didn't. Melody realized the shiver that had just raced up her spine was due to anticipation.

Norma Sue patted the chair beside her and Melody took it.

"So," she whispered. "How are you making it out there at Seth's?"

"Fine," Melody said, thinking about their argument from the afternoon. The less anyone knew about what was going on out at Seth's…. "It's a great place."

"We have a lot of ground to cover," Lacy called, saving Melody from further questions. "We just wanted to have this meeting and make sure everyone is on the same page about the booths for this weekend. The men have done a great job of marking off the booth space, and as you know, the vendors will start rolling into town on Thursday night."

Esther Mae waved her hand from the middle of the room. "Lacy, while I was gone did you find anyone to help work the dunking booth?"

"Sure did. Well, sort of. Applegate said he'd keep charge of the thing, so I found him a helper."

"So who'd you sucker into helping him?" Norma Sue asked. Leaning toward Melody she lowered her voice and added, "The poor helper usually has to climb up there and get dunked when no one else is around to do it."

"Melody!" Lacy chirped.

Esther Mae yelped in surprise as did the entire room.

"Me? No." She was certain that wasn't what Lacy had meant. The dunking booth would be the last place her friend would stick her…wouldn't it? The grin plastered across Lacy's face said differently.

"You said you'd help wherever I needed you."

"Yes. But, Lacy—"

Sheri, Lacy's partner in Heavenly Inspirations Hair Salon, leaned her chair back on two legs so she could see Melody. "You should know better than to give Lace that much freedom."

That got a round of happy agreements. True, Lacy was about as impetuous as they came, and Melody cringed. "I was thinking she might put me serving roasted peanuts or something!"

"That's a food booth. I told you, you were having fun this year, and the dunking booth is a blast."

"What would I need to do?"

"Sit on a little seat and wait to get bombed." Norma Sue chuckled.

"Oh, she will not," Lacy said, waving her pink-nailed fingers in the air. "You'll just hand the base-balls to the kids and the *cowboys* and tell them to hit the bull's-eye." Her electric-blue eyes sparkled. "That'll be much more fun than getting covered in spun sugar. Or smelling roasted like a peanut. Don't you think?"

"Yep. I'm putting you down with App. He'll take good care of you."

"That'll make her *into* a nut." Esther Mae harrumphed, and chuckles erupted throughout the room.

Melody decided thinking positive would be the best course. After all, Lacy really hadn't done it out of meanness but rather because she thought Melody would have fun. "I think he and I will get along just fine," she said. She liked Applegate although the older man had intimidated her when she first came to town. His gruff exterior and being hard of hearing had made her cringe. She'd thought he didn't like her at first but now she'd grown used to him and his bark was worse than his bite.

"Positive thinking. Good for you, Melody," Esther Mae said. "I think I might try and throw a ball at somebody this year."

"You don't throw the ball at somebody, Esther," Norma Sue said. "You hit a little bull's-eye. Hey, maybe we could get ole App to crawl up on that seat, and we could all take a turn dropping him into the water."

Lacy shook her head. "Oh, no, the name of this

game is to get good-looking *single cowboys* to sit up on that bulls-eye. That way the single girls can come spend their money to try and dunk them. Melody's being single and all was my reason for setting her up—I mean getting her to help. Who knows, Melody, Mr. Right might just be in the crowd this year."

Melody groaned inwardly. She'd escaped any matchmaking attempts so far. Her shyness had seemed to save her. But lately she'd been getting the idea that they were watching and getting ready to pounce on her. They just had to find the right point. She wasn't sure if this was a good time or not, but shyness wasn't considered a marriage-worthy quality, evidently.

By the time Melody walked out of the community center, she knew what was going on with every booth. And she was actually looking forward to the weekend.

She was halfway home when thoughts of Ty and Seth started crowding back into her thoughts.

Seth had been so adamant in taking up for her. It felt good to have someone thinking about her best interests like that. And yet she felt so defensive. He clearly wasn't happy with her when the rain had finally stopped. But he'd helped her leave the shelter of the overhang, and he'd carefully assisted her in getting up the hill. The horse was waiting not far from where they'd left him, and as she rode behind Seth out of the ravine she'd realized that treasure hunting hadn't crossed her mind since the rain had started. Seth Turner had.

Despite their disagreement, all she could think about was how safe he made her feel and that he was thinking about her well-being above all else.

Still he disagreed with how she handled her life.

But none of that stopped her from thinking about how tenderly he'd looked at her in the kitchen or how he took care of her in the storm. None of that could stop the way she felt when he looked at her or how she so much liked being in his arms. This was dangerous in every way, and she knew it. Falling for Seth was out of the question.

Not to mention again, that he was out of her league.

So out of her league, the matchmakers wouldn't even think to try and make a match of them. Even though she was out there right in the stagecoach house next door to him. Nope, no one would put a shy introvert with an outgoing, good-looking extrovert.

The idea was disturbing to her as she drove through the night.

## Chapter Thirteen

"Yah!" Seth shouted, cutting his horse into the path of the three heifers that had decided they didn't want to run with the crowd. John, the ranch border collie, charged from the back of the herd. Between Dough Boy's moves and John's moves, the heifers were scrambling to rejoin the group within moments.

And he was left to go back to his thoughts of Melody. It had probably been a good thing that he'd had to bow out of treasure hunting today. The ranch didn't run on its own and rounding up this group had required not only his participation and his hired hands' but that of several friends. The vet was due to arrive in an hour, and it would be a long day of shots and examinations.

"Thought you'd missed them," Jess, one of his

hands and a friend, called from across the herd as soon as Seth fell back into place. "You got something on your mind?"

"Just seeing if you're awake over there." That got him a laugh over the bawling cattle. Seth had a feeling a few friends had figured out his head was not in this section of the ranch.

He wondered if Melody had figured out just how badly he'd wanted to kiss her the day before. He also wondered if she'd had a call from her brother today, and if so, had she wired him the money he wanted or had she stood up for herself and said no more? It bothered him on all counts. For one, this was different…this feeling he had about Melody. This was deeper than anything he'd ever felt before. He'd only started to get to know her, but he couldn't stop thinking about her.

But this thing with her brother. He couldn't abide by it.

And why did he even think she cared whether he could or not? The only reason they ended the day on a good note was because he'd done as Melody wanted and they'd talked about the search for the treasure rather than the problem with her brother. His blood boiled just thinking about the creep using her the way he was. Sure, some would say he was sick, but from the little he'd learned about Ty Chandler, the man was unrepentant. Until the man took responsibility for his own actions, there wasn't anything Melody could do for the dude. Other than be his crutch.

"Hi, Seth. Goodness, you having a bad day?" the vet, Susan Worth, said coming around the back side of her truck.

"Nope. Not me." He was thinking positive.

"Liar." She shot him a teasing smile as she reached into the lockers on the side of her truck for her gear. "The scowl on your face tells the tale. You having woman trouble?"

He leaned against the truck and crossed his arms as he watched her. "Maybe," he confessed. "How's it going for you?"

She dropped a handful of syringes into her bag and leveled him with frank eyes. "Another one bites the dust. I'm about the unluckiest woman when it comes to love. But then, you already knew that, didn't you? We've had this conversation before."

"True." He and Susan had never dated though they'd bantered back and forth like they might one day. The timing just never seemed to be right. They never seemed to be dateless at the same time. He watched her working to organize the vaccines that she was about to use on his cattle.

He admired the graceful way her hands moved as she plucked bottles from their perch and deposited them into the bag. She was supermodel good-looking and had a killer personality. Men were crazy to let her get away. "We tend to repel relationships like water off a duck's back. We make a great pair don't we?" He chuckled at his stupid joke and was startled when she leaned a hip against the truck and looked up at him.

"Maybe we do," she said. "For the first time that I remember, it looks like we're both dateless at the same time."

She was standing mere inches from him, and her cinnamon eyes were dancing with flirtatious fire. His heart sank, knowing what she was expecting. The last thing he wanted to do was hurt Susan's feelings, but he was thinking about one woman right now and that was Melody.

"Seth," she urged, leaning closer, searching his eyes for a response. "Oh. So that's how it is. Anyone I know?"

He should have known Susan would take it in stride. "Maybe. But we're not dating."

"Yet."

"Not sure if she'll have me. Thanks for taking that so easy. You're a great gal, Susan." He felt like a jerk and knew he was saying everything wrong.

But what was he supposed to say? "I guess that sounds lame," he admitted.

She rolled her eyes. "Relax. They say dating is a numbers game...I've decided that my number got left out of the bingo cage."

"A smart man's gonna come along and surprise you one of these days, so hang in there."

She shot him a doubtful look then winked. "Don't forget me if this one doesn't work out," she said teasingly then headed toward the squeeze chute where the first cow was waiting.

Seth followed her. Susan was a strong woman. He didn't tell her but he'd heard from several ex-dates of hers that the guys just couldn't compete with that. He personally thought it was a very attractive trait for a woman.

He was attracted to the strength he'd glimpsed in Melody. She'd been through so much, as with-drawn as she was, and yet she held it together. Melody was stronger than she thought she was. All she needed was to find the confidence to stand up to her brother.

"This could be it," Melody said on Thursday. She'd been disappointed when Seth had to cancel treasure hunting the day before to work cattle. She hadn't been able to convince herself that it didn't have something to do with their disagreement over Ty. She reminded herself that the man did have a ranch to run.

She'd thrown herself into her research, hoping to lose herself in trying to figure out who the mystery man was. But so far nothing else made sense. Sure it might not have been Nixon or Davis, and this might not be their share of the sixty thousand in gold coins. But they still remained her front-runners.

"I have racked my brain and to me this is what I consider the best bet for matching rocks. Even if this is the north end of the ravine and not the south."

"Who knows, he might have been directionally challenged like me," she said.

They hadn't mentioned Ty today, and she got the feeling Seth was trying hard to mind his own business. She found that endearing, which was dangerous for her to be thinking. Not to mention that she was trying not to think about Ty in any capacity today. He hadn't called the day before or this morning, and that actually caused her to wonder what was going on…which was crazy. But she hadn't sent him the money and she—she yanked a mental blackout curtain down between her and any thoughts about him. Seth would be proud of her if he could read her thoughts. At least she thought he would.

She refocused on thinking about the treasure map.

"It's easy to get disoriented in here," Seth was saying. "Even for the not-so-challenged."

She couldn't help but smile. "I could take that as an insult," she said.

Seth laughed, and the sound filled her with longing and her attempt to ignore her attraction for him flew out the window—or flew up in the air since she was outside.

Treasure. She was supposed to only be thinking about treasure today.

Taking a deep breath, she turned west. Seth raised a teasing brow when he saw that she had indeed turned the right direction.

"I'm going to learn my directions before this is all said and done," she said.

"Hey," he chuckled. "I have faith in you."

She liked the sound of that far too much. "Here goes," she said, and started walking off the steps. The ground wasn't as overgrown with underbrush on this side of the ravine. There was more rock and she was pretty certain less clay. And that meant, at least to her, that where there was more rock there was more chance of a cave. At twenty-five steps, as they'd done before, she paused to look for anything that suggested towers, but there was nothing so she continued on.

"Fifty!" she exclaimed finally. "Do you see anything?" She didn't.

He shook his head. "What did the dude mean?" Seth mumbled almost to himself, frustrated. "By this ridiculous map, there should be something right here, if this is the spot."

But there wasn't anything. Melody's mood plummeted. She'd been trying so hard to keep her spirits up. "What else could it be? Either we have the wrong place or we have hit upon the worst treasure-map maker in all of history."

She sank to a small rock in order to keep herself from stomping her foot like a three-year-old. "I just knew this was the right side when I saw that the ground was more rocky. The real south corner over where we were the day before yesterday was more clay. I mean, that's logical. Isn't it?"

Seth nodded, still searching. "I was an idiot not to think of it then." He rubbed the back of his neck and turned to stare back at the way they'd come. Then he swung around and hit her with skeptical eyes. "Okay, what-if. And this is a big what-if. But, maybe, just maybe, we have it all wrong. Maybe our guy wasn't so stupid after all. Maybe he wrote the map so that he could figure it out and no one else could."

"But then why would he have given it to your

grandfather? I mean, wouldn't that be kind of mean for him to send your grandfather, the man who was trying to help him get well, on a wild-goose chase?"

"Maybe he didn't give the map to him. Maybe he died with it in his pocket. I don't get it either but what if south is north and west is east? Maybe the dude was easily confused and didn't do it on purpose. We will never know unless we at least give it a shot." He lifted a brow as if to question if she was game.

She stood up. "So you're saying that back there is the right spot to start but we need to go east now instead of west?"

"That's my best shot."

"Then let's go. I've got nothing better."

She scooted past him and practically ran back the fifty feet to the boulders.

"Whoa, woman," he called when she stumbled on a root. "I don't want you banging up your other knee."

That had been the first thing he'd asked about that morning. But she'd assured him that though her knee was a bit sore, the cut hadn't really been too bad. Still, just remembering how careful he'd been looking after it and then how sweet he'd been carrying her up the hill made that ache return to her heart. "I'll be careful," she said and hurried the rest of the way to the boulders. Once there, she wasted no time, just started counting as she headed east. It was quickly apparent that going this way followed the path of the river as it snaked through the ravine. And even before she reached the count of fifty she could tell there was no tower. There was only trees and overgrowth similar to what they'd found on the other side of the ravine.

"So much for my bright idea," Seth muttered.

Melody sighed when she'd rather scream. Turning around, she stared at him. "It's a wonder your grandfather didn't go crazy doing this."

"I actually think he might have just a bit. I mean, think about it—evidently this is what the man did. He roamed these woods while his wife and son worked hard to keep up the stage stop. I think that's not only crazy but unforgivable. Coming into this, I didn't have a favorable image of him. Now I certainly don't." He glared about him, clearly aggravated.

"Maybe he had stars in his eyes, because he thought if he found the money he'd be able to give his family an easier life? Maybe he was really a good guy who just lost his way?"

He stared at her anger flashing in his eyes. "You really need to get rid of this soft spot you have about men who mistreat women."

"Seth—"

He cut her off. "First, you're too easy on your brother and now you're trying to give my sorry grandfather the easy way out. The truth is your brother owes you a ton of apologies. And my ancestor owes his wife and son the same."

"You are cold-blooded," Melody snapped, going defensive before she could even think not to.

His eyes darkened. "*I'm* cold-blooded? Why, because I expect a man to stand up and be a man? I don't think so."

Melody closed her eyes and let the anger churn through her like a wildfire eating up dry grass. Why was she so angry with Seth? "I didn't mean that," she said, at last. "I'm sorry."

"Melody, I'm just trying to make you see the light."

He couldn't help it if he didn't understand. She knew that. People who hadn't walked this path with someone they loved couldn't understand the emotions that went with it. "I know you are," she said. And she was drawn to him because he was trying to look out for her best interests. But at the same time she knew this was a wedge that couldn't be overcome between them. Not deeply, not in ways that could ever let them be more than friends.

She blinked hard at the sudden dampness that

thought brought to her. Looking away, she pretended to scan the area when what she was really doing was buying her silly emotions time to get right. How many times did she have to remind herself that even daydreaming about Seth was ridiculous? She was staring unseeingly at a clump of bushes that was blurred through the tears that remained pooled in her eyes. Needing to sniff but not daring to for fear Seth would hear it and realize she was crying, instead she took a deep breath and blinked hard to clear her vision…and that's when she realized what her gaze had fixated on.

"Seth," she gasped. "What is that?" She pointed into the bushes a little way up the incline.

"What?"

"There, those rocks. See?" She grabbed his arm and practically yanked him off his feet as she pointed into the bushes. "There."

He bent beside her. "Well, what do ya know."

In the bushes was a pile of rocks that looked like they'd been carefully piled by hand. Around them were other stones that looked as if they'd toppled from the stack over time. She turned her face toward his. "Do you think it's the tower? Because I know it's not a big tower, or towering trees or towering rocks. But still they're stacked up."

He straightened up and grinned down at her.

"One man's stack is another man's tower. And that looks like a tower to me. It could have made it all this time hidden like that and with so little traffic out here."

Melody screamed with excitement, which was so unlike her, and then deviated more from the norm by slinging her arms around Seth. This was so not happening to her! She was ecstatic as she jumped up and down like a *Price Is Right* contestant before getting hold of herself. Still clinging to him, she looked back at the stack. "Just think, oh, my goodness, *just think*—those stones may have been sitting there stacked by our mystery man for over a hundred years." It was too much to imagine. For a history teacher it was an amazing idea. But for a history buff it was unbelievable! "What was the rest of the map? My head is spinning, and I just can't remember," she said. She was absolutely giddy.

"Begin south corner ravine at the matching rocks. Fifty steps west to tower turn twenty-five degrees left. At the rock follow the crust to the cave," Seth quoted the words he'd memorized. "So, twenty-five degrees to the left should mean we're going right. It doesn't say how far to the rock, but I'm guessing it's a big enough or distinctive enough rock so it must not have needed more.

Especially since it must be near something that looks like crust."

"That's the weird part," Melody said, searching.

Seth lined up with the rocks and then turned slightly. "The problem is he doesn't say where to be facing when you establish your twenty-five degree turn."

"I guess he didn't want to make it easy on anyone if he wasn't going to be the one to find it."

He raised a brow. "Evidently. But, through those trees is the river. And there is a rock area so from where I'm standing right now that's where we'll end up, and I think that's our best starting point."

"Then let's go that way."

Seth led the way. Melody scrambled behind him feeling so keyed up her hands were shaking.

When she saw the rock, she knew they'd solved the map. There was a rocky ledge that jutted out from the earth and disappeared around a curve that followed the line of the river below. It was not more than two feet wide, and it looked like the crisp edge of a pie crust. Melody thought it was an odd comparison for a man to make, but it worked. There was no doubt about it. Below them was the river and behind them the ravine sloped gradually away from the ledge. Seth was busy stomping down some brush so that they could see better what they were dealing with. She wondered if his heart was pumping as rapidly as hers. She'd never in a million years dreamed when she'd taken the chance and called his ranch that day to ask if she could tour the stagecoach house that it would lead to her actually finding a buried treasure. Of course she hadn't found the treasure yet, but it almost felt as if they had.

After considerable stomping, Seth turned to her and held out his hand. "I feel like a kid," he said, giving a cute little laugh that made her feel like there were a thousand children doing cartwheels inside her heart.

She took his hand and knew her heart had just crossed a dangerous boundary she had no business crossing.

"We're supposed to follow this. Now watch your footing. This could get tricky. I don't want you falling and hurting yourself."

She nodded but knew it was already too late for that.

## Chapter Fourteen

Seth held tightly to Melody's hand as he followed the rock ledge. It wasn't really dangerous but one misstep and a person could fall off the ledge, hit the ground the short four feet below the ledge and then roll or slide over the edge into the river. He wasn't about to take a chance on Melody taking that ride. She'd seemed to get her footing better today than the other days but still, all it would take was one slipup.

And the fact that they were both excited about the possibility of finding the cave and the treasure was an added liability when it came to keeping their feet planted firmly on the ground.

Seeing the sparkle in her eyes was enough to send him skydiving.

They reached the edge, and Melody's grip tightened on his. He realized that he wanted to find the treasure more for the pleasure it would give her than anything. The area was overgrown like everything else but sloping back away from the rock ledge. But there was nothing else there. At least not visible.

Melody sighed. "I guess I was expecting the cave opening to just be right here. Instead, the rock disappeared, and it looks like everything else."

The disappointment was heavy in her voice. "C'mon now," he said, gently hugging her. "You've pushed and prodded me for days. Don't go giving up so quickly. We've come this far, and there is no doubt in my mind that that map has led us somewhere important. We just have to keep looking till we find it." She looked up at him and nodded.

"You're right. I'm just anxious."

"Me, too. Let's start looking for anything around here that could be a cave opening. And, remember, that could be a hole only big enough for a person to squeeze through, or a hole in the ground, so watch your step. Not all caves are yawning openings that you can just waltz through."

"I'm ready. I've thought about the cave and prayed it would be big. I'm not a spelunker—isn't that what they call the guys who crawl around in the caves like otters?"

*Otters.* Cute. "Right. Of course a more experienced explorer is called a caver. You ever seen those bumper stickers that say Cavers Rescue Spelunkers?"

"Wow. Where did all that come from?"

He gave a shrug. "What can I say? Like I told you, I dreamed of finding treasure when I was a kid. And to me, any good treasure should be buried in a cave. So I did my research."

Her chuckle warmed his heart. "Okay, you'll have to fill me in on this more. But for now let's try and make that dream come true."

"Fine by me." Before letting her loose to search, he gave her another one-armed hug and fought the want to pull her close and kiss her smiling lips. "Careful, okay?"

He moved toward the largest mass of vegetation and peered into it. He'd tromped this ravine like Lewis and Clark when he'd been a kid. The idea that there was indeed a cave here and he'd missed it didn't give him much hope in his skills as a spelunker, much less a caver. Still, this was a huge area, and the undergrowth was dense so he gave himself a bit of slack. He glanced to where Melody was also pushing and pulling at a mass of grapevine and yaupon. "Watch for snakes," he warned.

"Hey!" She shot him a glare and jumped back. "I'm trying not to think about them, and so far that's held them at bay all this time. Don't start talking about them now."

He grinned. "I'm sorry to remind you, but it's just so you don't stick your hand somewhere that it shouldn't be."

She pulled both hands back and scanned the massive tangle of vines overlaying the bushes. "Maybe we need a machete or something."

He pushed further into the bushes he was investigating, feeling the ground slope up beneath his boots. "Not a bad idea. Maybe we should call it quits today and bring back some equipment tomorrow."

"No—I mean, it's only four o'clock. We still have daylight for a few hours," she said but stopped digging around in the vines and walked to stand beside him.

He figured they needed tools but gave the vines he was grasping a hard yank and then went still. Beside him Melody did the same, obviously seeing the same shadow far back in the foliage. She looked up at him with wide violet eyes.

He smiled. "I think we're going to need some light. What about you?"

"So, I'll pack a lunch, and we'll plan to spend the entire day again," Melody said as they pulled up in front of the stagecoach house a couple hours later. She'd chattered all the way home. Poor Seth probably wanted to *run.*

He laid his arm across the back of the seat. "Sounds like a plan."

"Great. I can't wait. Do you want to come in for a glass of tea or I could make a pot of coffee?" She didn't want him to leave yet. Actually she didn't want to get out of the truck.

"Sure," he said. "Then I'll head home and get our gear together for tomorrow."

Melody led the way into the house, and as always, especially since it had been a couple of days since she'd heard from Ty, her gaze sought out the answering machine. The light was blinking, and she hesitated, her heart torn. "Tea or coffee?" she asked, walking to the kitchen.

"Tea," Seth said.

As she reached inside the refrigerator for the pitcher of cold tea, she saw him pause at the answering machine. "My head is still spinning from the thoughts that tomorrow we might find something." She grabbed glasses and tried to ignore the fact that he was probably wondering the same thing she was—whether the blinking light was from Ty.

He crossed the room and took the tea but set it on the counter. "Tomorrow is going to be a big day, and I think I better go on back to the house and get things ready."

Melody didn't want him to leave. "If you think that's best."

He didn't make a move for the door, and it was more than obvious that something was on his mind. "That blinking light."

Her stomach hurt. She didn't want to talk about the light. Or Ty. Not tonight.

"Is that who I think it is?"

"Seth, let's not start—"

"Look, I can't help it. Does he call you every day of the year?"

"No. Not *every* day." She set her tea down and started to turn away but Seth took her shoulders.

"Melody, I'm not asking this to get you all uptight. I've tried to keep out of it. But that has to wear on you."

She sighed. "It does."

"Did you send him the money?"

"No."

"Good for you," he said, and then he pulled her into his arms and kissed her on the temple.

Melody couldn't say it was exactly the kiss or the moment she'd been daydreaming about. It was actually about the worst atmosphere for a kiss she could have imagined. She pushed out of Seth's arms. "You know what? It's been a long day, and I'm pretty tired."

"Sure," he said. "I'll see you early."

"I'll be ready." She watched him leaving and waited as he closed the door behind him. She didn't move but stood there listening as his boot steps receded.

She should have been ecstatic about the next day, but she suddenly felt empty. She looked at the floor and all her research papers stacked neatly around her. This had been her escape…but she hadn't escaped anything. Instead she'd run head-first into a wreck. She felt tangled inside. Seth said he was concerned about her, and he was saying things she'd thought herself. She knew she needed to let Ty find his own way. She'd been trying to figure it out. So why did she feel so resentful every time Seth voiced his thoughts? His simple stare at the blinking light bothered her.

It seemed like her whole world was made up of questions these days. And if she stayed busy she could sometimes not think about the fact that she had no answers.

She'd always had a strong faith in God. She'd been taught early that God was always there for her and she'd seen her parents' faith carry them through so many hard times. Always, they'd trusted that the Lord was in control. And she believed that, too.

She was just struggling with understanding the why of it all.

She knew she wasn't the only person in America who had problems. And sadly she understood that the nightmare of drug abuse was widespread and growing. Feeling sorry for herself was not what she wanted to feel. But sometimes she felt so alone. So isolated. She'd thought talking to Seth would help her. She'd actually prayed that God would give her some answers. That He would hear her prayers, know that she was angry and desperate…it was almost her last-ditch effort to believe that God hadn't just given up on Ty but that He'd also not given up on her.

*Stop it*. Melody rubbed her temple, her gaze falling on the blinking red light. Letting these emotions get a grip on her wasn't good. She needed to shake it off. But she'd really thought, well, she and Seth had become something over the last three weeks—she wasn't exactly sure what that was but it was something. Maybe it was simply that they'd spent so much time together that she'd opened up to him like she'd never opened up to anyone before. And, in turn, he felt comfortable giving her advice.

Only, did she want that advice? Instead of feeling less isolated she felt...depressed.

So depressed that she did something she'd never done before. She walked over and unplugged her phone. Then staring at the blinking red light she snapped the answering machine off.

She just couldn't face talking to her brother—not tonight.

## Chapter Fifteen

Friday was a beautiful day for spelunking. Melody had been outside waiting on Seth when he drove up. She'd been determined that today she was not going to let problems weigh her down.

She'd also left her phone unplugged, but she wasn't going to think about *that* either.

"You're in a good mood this morning," Seth said as she jumped into the front seat, depositing the small cooler with their sandwiches in the seat.

"I am. So don't mess it up." She shot him a warning look. "Now, hit the road, Jack. We have a treasure to find."

Seth gave her a curious look but put the truck in gear. "I've got us packed up and ready for an all-dayer."

"Sounds great."

They small talked all the way to the ravine. She was glad he had taken her hint and was going to keep the conversation on neutral ground…that was part of the reason she'd been waiting outside for him, not wanting him to see that her phone or answering machine were unplugged. Today was about the quest, and she didn't need him asking questions or judging her actions.

Since they knew where the cave was, Seth was able to park the truck in a location at the top of the ravine that would minimize their hike. Instead of bringing Dough Boy, he'd brought a backpack. As they unloaded and he pulled down the tailgate she surveyed the assortment of gear. Lights, a couple of shovels, rope. She looked at the rope. "Surely we won't have to use that. I mean, our guy was an 1800s cowboy on a horse and he was sick."

Seth pulled the backpack on and grinned at her. "I seriously doubt we're going to have to use it, but it never hurts to be prepared."

"You're right," she said, pulling the strap of the small cooler over her head and situating the square container so that it hung at the small of her back. "So I don't get a backpack?"

"Not today. Like you said, the dude was on a horse. I'm expecting that if he buried the treasure, it's somewhere near the opening. That means I don't think we're going to need to test our limited spelunking techniques much." He grabbed a shovel and handed her one. "You can carry that," he said while he picked up a machete in a sheath and clipped it onto his belt.

This was it. They really were about to hack their way through a tangle of yaupon and vines and enter a cave that had maybe not been explored by anyone in over a hundred years. She got goose bumps.

Seth led the way, and it took them less than an hour to make it to the ledge. But since he now knew where the cave was Seth was able to lead in a quicker way, bypassing the walk along the ledge. "This was so much easier," she said.

"Yeah. It's a lot easier to find when it's not hidden in a backward map." He set his backpack down and slid the machete out of its holder. "Stand back while I get rid of this."

He didn't have to tell her twice. She watched as he expertly wielded the sharp blade. She watched the muscles in his arms and back bunch and stretch with each swing of the machete. Her insides melted watching him work. The morning was already hot even though it was only about ten o'clock, but she shivered remembering the feel of those arms each time he'd pulled her close. He paused to swipe perspiration from his brow with his forearm and caught her watching him. He winked and went back to work.

Her heart hammered in her chest as if she'd been the one swinging the machete. It didn't take too long for him to have a path cut to the rocks, and sure enough—just as they'd believed—there was a slim opening. "Amazing," Seth said, sheathing the machete as he leaned into the crevice for a first look.

Melody was right behind him carrying the backpack. She set it on the ground and pulled out the lights. Her fingers trembled doing so.

"I'll go first. I'm thinking I've made enough noise to scare off anything hiding inside, but just in case let's take it nice and slow."

"Gotcha," Melody agreed. Texas had an abundance of wildlife, including snakes—rattlers and copperheads, to be specific—and she prayed again that none of them was waiting to ambush them inside the cave. Out in the woods everything had the chance to hear them coming and had gotten out of their way before they had any encounters. But this was a cave. "Be careful."

"If I get hurt, are you going to be my nurse?"

The teasing question startled her. "Maybe," she teased back.

"Maybe isn't much incentive for a guy to put

everything on the line for," he said, his voice a low rumble as he seemed to lean closer in her direction. "Come here."

She stepped forward. Her insides had gone to complete mush. "I—I would be your nurse," she said, but it came out as a whisper. A cracked whisper, like she'd been stranded in the desert without water for days.

He didn't touch her—just leaned forward. As her stomach and heart seemed to knock together, he touched his lips to hers. The erratic knock of her heart thumping and banging surely could be heard as he kissed her. This was not the kiss on the temple like the day before. This was toe curling, lose-your-heart kind of dangerous. And when he pulled away, he looked as shaken as she felt. She blinked and tried to stop her world from spinning but she knew that was probably not going to happen.

If she'd ever wondered what it would feel like to hop on that mechanical bull, she didn't need to wonder any longer. She was so there. And so in trouble. Because she had no idea what she was doing...

What was he doing? Seth practically stumbled away from Melody. The dazed look in her amethyst eyes and the feel of her lips scorching his skin very nearly knocked him to his knees. All night long he'd fought his feelings for her. It would be easy to love Melody—but implementing and sustaining that love when the issue of her brother was concerned wasn't likely something they could come to a compromise about. It had taken all his willpower so far this morning not to ask if she'd called him back.

He'd known kissing her was a dangerous step that he needed to stay clear of at all costs. But here he'd gone and done it anyway.

He stepped into the cave. Taking a deep breath of the cool, dank air, he let his eyes adjust. As he directed the flashlight beam about the cavern, he saw that it wasn't terribly big. But there was room to stand, and there would have been room for a man his size to stretch out on the floor without having to curl up in the center area. He walked forward and shined his light into another opening. This room was dark, cut off from the slight light source the outside opening provided, and it was much larger.

"Seth."

He took a deep breath. He wasn't sure what was happening between them, but he knew he was getting in way over his head. If it was just about them, he'd be all gung ho about the way she tore him up inside…it was a good feeling. But there was her brother to contend with. And his gut told him he'd better tread lightly.

"You can come in," he called. "All's clear." *He wished.*

Her gasp filled the cavern, and he couldn't help smiling at the look of amazement that lit her eyes.

"Oh, Seth, this is so awesome."

She was awesome. This was just a cave. "You might want to look through here," he said indicating the next opening. She smiled, and the slight hesitancy in her step, as if not sure she should get close to him, was the only thing that made him think she was still thinking about the kiss. He stepped back, giving her wider berth. She took the opening and moved past him, shining her light into the next room.

"Oh, wow!"

Looking at her profile, Seth knew exactly how she felt.

Melody didn't know if it was the fact that she was fulfilling so many dreams by standing inside this cave—feeling like she was discovering history versus just teaching it—or that she was standing beside Seth that her knees were still shaking from the kiss that he'd given her.

There was nothing about her life that wasn't complicated. Everything was running on parallels. She had the depression and hardship of dealing with all things Ty running on one track. On another track she had the thrill of discovering the treasure map. The thrill of discovering this cave and maybe, just maybe, having the thrill of discovering a treasure that had been long buried and actually becoming a part of what that find would represent in the vast, rich fullness of Texas history. It was amazing to her. But on the last track, there was the runaway train that was her emotional attachment to Seth…it was still hard for her to believe that he could possibly be interested in her on the same level that she felt about him.

"You ready?" His voice brushed across her neck as he leaned close behind her.

She turned her head slightly, bringing her face close to his. In the light of the flashlight, his brown eyes searched hers. She swallowed, wishing for things she couldn't let herself voice. "Yes," she whispered. "Let's do this," she said more strongly, grabbing her emotions by the throat. Moving away from him, she hurried outside for the shovels while he tugged open the backpack and pulled out a high-beam lantern.

"Oh, that will help," she said.

"It's rechargeable. I keep a few of them on hand on the ranch for emergencies." He looked boyish as he turned the lantern on and smiled at her when the light came to life. "We should be able to see anything hidden above ground with this."

Melody rolled her eyes. "I do believe I may have awakened a sleeping giant."

"Oh, yeah. Stick with me, kid, and if there's treasure to be found we'll find it."

"Lead on." She laughed, grabbing her shovel and waving him forward. "Although, I was reading about caves and exploring and such. We aren't really supposed to touch things. So maybe digging is out of the question."

He stopped and looked over his shoulder at her. "Are you serious?"

"Well, that's just what I read."

He continued on inside the cave with her following at his heels. "I've read all of that, too. But see, that's all that stuff with letting folks in on my business. This is my land, and as far as I'm concerned, you and I will be the only two folks ever to set foot in here." He grinned. "We can pretty much do what we want to do." He set the lantern down and placed his hands on his hips as he surveyed the brightly lit cavern.

"You're serious?"

"You bet I'm serious. I'm all for preserving history, but you won't ever change my mind about my right not to alert the masses if I have a part of that history on my private land."

They both began walking the cave looking for any obvious signs that something had been disturbed. There were different sized rocks and various nooks and crannies where saddlebags could very easily have been stuffed. Melody shined her light inside one such opening and saw nothing so she moved on to the next one. "What if everyone felt the way you do?"

"What if?"

She couldn't believe him. "Honestly, Seth. What about stewardship?"

His chuckle bounced off the walls. "I think my way of thinking is great stewardship."

"But—"

"But what?"

"You are exasperating." She shined her light into a hole and thought she saw the flash of eyes. Probably a raccoon or possum—whatever it was, Melody moved on quickly.

"I could say the same thing about you."

"Then I guess we're on the same page," she said and hoped he didn't start up about Ty. If he did, she was just going to tell him to mind his own business. She could handle this on her own. She'd decided that having someone to confide in was overrated, and she'd rather go back to the way it was when no one from Mule Hollow knew about her brother.

Seth's jaw muscle jerked as he stared at her, and his dark eyes reflected the lantern light like a mirror. Turning away, Melody grabbed the lantern and strode toward the interior room. She felt pretty certain that if treasure was to be found above ground it would be there. Normally, striding off into dark places wasn't on her list of things okay to do. But at the moment that seemed safer than waiting for Seth to start up a dialogue about her brother.

In the second cavern, the ceiling wasn't much taller but it gradually rose as it receded into the shadows that the lantern light didn't reach. Melody held the lantern higher, and it bathed the rock in a golden light. "I think I could get used to this," she said as Seth entered the cavern.

"It is pretty cool," he said. "And if I keep this place a secret, it could be another two hundred years before someone else comes in here and disturbs it. But if word—"

Melody swung toward him. "Yes, if word gets out about the map, no telling how many loonies will be out here swamping the place and painting graffiti on the walls as they dig for the treasure."

"It could happen."

She threw her head back and stared at the ceiling in exasperation. The man didn't want folks on his property, but was he teasing her? She looked at him and shook her head. "Sometimes you drive me crazy."

He smiled and started walking the room slowly, flashing his light the same way he'd done before. They worked this way for several minutes.

"Is something bothering you today?"

"Bothering me?" She glanced at him. He was studying the ground behind a row of rocks.

"Yeah, you think I haven't noticed?"

"Well, um…"

"You shouldn't, you know. Feel bad, that is."

"I don't know what we're doing here. We should just rent a metal detector and be done with this." She hated the way his words made her feel.

"You feel guilty because you're who you are. Your brother may be sick like you think, but he also doesn't have to try and help himself because you give him a crutch."

"If we leave now, we can call and find a metal detector this afternoon and be back out here tomorrow to wrap up this mystery once and for all."

Melody headed for the exit, ready to get away from Seth and the conversation he insisted they have. She didn't want to have it. She didn't want to talk about this. Or think about it. What she'd wanted was to hunt for treasure. To lose herself in the hunt and pretend—she stopped walking and hung her head as she studied her dusty boots. Her blood pounded like freighters out of control, making her dizzy with the strain. She lifted her palms to heated cheeks and tried to will herself to calm down before she either fainted or turned around and said something she really didn't want to say. Seth had no right to push like this.

"You have no right," she said, her voice so low she almost didn't hear it over the turmoil in her head.

"I can't not think about this. Did you think I couldn't tell that you were upset this morning? Look at you. You're pale, you have circles under your eyes like you didn't sleep. And I'm betting the lack of sleep isn't something new. The thing is, I get where you're coming from. You're a wonderful, sweet and giving woman. Of course you want to give everything you have for your brother. The crazy jerk doesn't know what he's throwing away. He's so selfish, and at this point, I'm sure it's the drugs doing his thinking for him. But you're letting him continue, and you have to stop. And I can't help trying to make you see that."

"Why is that? Why does this matter so much to you, Seth? I don't get this. You barely know me. You have no one close to you with this problem and yet you think you have all the answers. Well, you don't. It just isn't as easy as you think."

"Why not? Maybe it's not as hard as you think."

"You aren't emotionally involved. That's why. You don't know what it's like to see your older brother go from being the person you idolize into being somebody you don't recognize anymore. I mean, yes, he's horrible now, a total jerk and yes, he uses me. And sometimes I—" She could hardly breathe as anger violently swept through her in a hot rush. Her chest heaved, her hands shook and her mouth was dry with the need to vomit. And tears—she had to grit the tears back for fear once they started she would shatter with the force of them. Oh, she hated this!

She raised her hand to her face then dropped it to her side before lifting a finger to silence the words she could see forming behind his somewhat shocked expression. "You—" her lips trembled, as did her voice "—you. Have. No idea. *No* idea how I feel. The truth. I want to know what my parents did to deserve a life of constant stress and strain watching their child struggle with something they couldn't fix. Something they tried so hard to fix, spending everything they had and more on the quest. And always. Always trusting that God was going to fix him. And for what? For God to totally ignore their faithful prayers?"

"Melody—"

"No." She held her hand up to silence him. "No. You wanted to know so bad—well, here it is. I've done everything like my parents. I've prayed the prayers until I don't believe them anymore. I pay his way. *I'm* the good daughter by doing what my mom asked of me. But I resent it and I feel guilty, yes. I feel guilty for everything. I can't win. I feel guilty that it's not me who has the problem. I mean, really, why Ty? Why not me? And believe me, he's thought the very same thing. I feel guilty that I hate what he's done to my life. I feel guilty about all of it. It's a no-win situation for me, and I hate it. But here's the kicker of all kickers. I'm so angry at God I can hardly think straight sometimes. I mean…" she gasped for breath and placed a hand on her stomach as she felt ill. It had become unbearably hot, and she knew it was from the emotions raging inside of her. "I mean my parents believed and prayed that God would heal Ty. They did everything they could for him. And

God let them down. Until this moment I don't think I realized just how angry I am at God. I feel like He's lied to me. To my parents. We've done everything we could. We've trusted Him and for what?" She had to get out of the cave. This was no longer fun. She was suffocating. She stumbled through into the outer cave and practically ran out into the open air. She stumbled and fell to her knees on the hard earth, and the tears that she'd fought off came out in a rush.

She didn't know Seth was beside her until he pulled her into his arms. She hit his chest with her fist and cried fierce sobs. He let her pound his chest and then he gently cupped her head to his shoulder as she wept.

"Let it all out," he whispered against her hair. Slowly the world stopped spinning and her sobs subsided to sniffles. His shirt was soaked against her cheek. She was drained, and her head felt like it had sledgehammers pounding away inside of it.

She knew she should apologize for her outburst but she didn't have it in her to do so. "I need to get home," was all she said as she pushed out of Seth's arms.

"I'll get the stuff," he said, but she wasn't listening.

## Chapter Sixteen

Seth never felt so terrible in all of his life. He'd pushed Melody until she'd broken. As they rode in silence back to the stagecoach house, he was at a loss as to how to comfort her.

She'd been honest, and she'd been right. He'd never walked in her shoes before, so who was he to tell her how to run her life?

*You're the man who loves her.* It was true. As he held her while she cried, he'd known there was no turning back for him. He loved Melody with a love every bit as fierce as the emotions that were streaming out of her. While her heart was pouring out in anguish, all he'd wanted to do was fill her heart back up with enough love to wipe away all the sadness and the pain. She'd had all that anger bottled up for years and she'd been alone. He was no expert; he didn't know what advice a medical professional would give her, but he knew one thing…and he wondered if she'd ever considered it. The words weighing heavy on his heart were words that could very well ruin any chance he might have to ever have a life with Melody.

In the distance he saw the stagecoach house. Sturdy, built to last the test of time. *Dear Lord, give me something,* he prayed, feeling the weight of Melody's grief on his shoulders. He loved her. But could he help her?

*Yes.*

He didn't want to tell her but he knew he was supposed to…the crazy pieces of this puzzle they were living hadn't just fallen into place accidentally. Her being here on his property where he could overhear her conversation with Ty and see the pain it was causing her was for a reason. She was too close to her brother to see reason. She was right that he'd never walked in her shoes, but he could clearly see that the path she was treading was not good for her. He had to speak up and help her move forward.

He could lose her forever.

*Trust me.*

He pulled to a halt. "Are you going to be okay?"

Her breath rattled as she inhaled. She didn't look at him but nodded.

Her skin was pale and her eyes were dull. She didn't look okay. "Melody," he said clearing his throat, his fingers gripping the steering wheel so tightly his knuckles whitened. *He would lose her.* "Let me drive you to the festival in the morning. I have to work it, too. No sense us both—"

"No, thank you. I want to drive myself," she said, and then she got out of the truck and walked away.

Coward. He'd felt God urging him to trust Him. To speak what was in his heart. But he hadn't done it. Seth snatched his hat off his head and threw it across the cab, watching it slam into the dash and fall to the floorboard. "How am I supposed to tell her she needs to trust You when I can't do it myself?"

Not with Melody. Not with someone he loved so much.

Mule Hollow knew how to put on a festival. Melody had driven up and parked at the far end of town because even at nine, with the festival scheduled to start at ten, there were cars everywhere. She hadn't come to town the day before but knew that it had been alive with vendors getting ready for the morning. Many of the vendors had included Mule Hollow on their schedule and were "repeat offenders" as Sheriff

Brady liked to call them. This year was the first time in a long time that Mule Hollow actually had not only Sheriff Brady on hand but a deputy to help him, ex-Texas Ranger Zane Cantrell. It was a real sign that the town was growing when it could begin to expand its law enforcement. Not that there was a high crime rate or anything like that. It was just nice that Sheriff Brady could have a little time off now that he and his wife, Dottie, had their first baby.

Babies were the agenda these days—almost more than matchmaking. Melody had a feeling that soon Lacy would be announcing that she and Clint were expecting their first child. And she thought that would be just wonderful.

Positive things.

She'd been trying to think about positive things ever since her emotional breakdown the day before. She'd walked inside after leaving Seth and gone straight to her room and crawled into bed. She'd fallen asleep at some point and been thankful for the peace she found there. She'd begun to wonder if she would ever truly know peace.

She knew the peace of understanding that because of her decision to trust the Lord as her savior that she had the peace of everlasting life… but that didn't mean she never had questions or doubts. Or that she never got angry at God. She was dealing right now in the best way that she knew how.

And in dealing she hoped she didn't see much of Seth today.

The man had pushed her to her limit and then he'd held her like she meant something to him. The emotions she felt for him on top of everything else in her life were just too much to deal with.

Taking a deep breath, she got out of her car and walked toward the vacant field on the far side of Sam's Diner. She walked past Adela's family home. It was a huge Victorian house with green turrets. This was home to Melody. She felt comfortable here in this beautiful little town. She felt more peace here than she'd ever felt…but she was living a lie. Here she'd tried to ignore who she really was.

She walked down the street past Adela's then on down past Heavenly Inspirations Hair Salon, past Ashby's Treasures, Dottie's Candies. Farther down the street sat Prudy's Garage, and it still boasted the red flying horse from an era when stations were full service. Life here in this town just seemed to have a quality of timelessness. But Melody felt like her time was running out. She had to figure out what she was going to do about her life.

Hiding out, pretending that she didn't have a brother with problems hadn't worked. Burying herself in research and even a treasure hunt hadn't gotten her any further along.

She felt like a hamster running and running and running and going nowhere. All this time, all these years, and she was moving as fast as she could, but she hadn't moved an inch.

She was in crisis. Were Christians supposed to have crises? Of faith, of joy?

"Melody, yoo-hoo, Melody," Esther Mae called from her car. "Can you help me?"

Glad to have something else to focus on, Melody jogged across the street and grabbed the crate of cookies the beaming redhead was just about to drop because she was trying to carry too much. Melody knew the feeling.

"Goodness, God's timing was perfect for sending you to help me!" Esther Mae exclaimed.

Melody fumbled to get a better grip on the crate. "Wow," she said, looking down at the gold mine of cookies. "Did you make all of these yourself?"

"I did, and thanks to you they're not going to be a jumble in the middle of Main Street. I've been baking for three days."

Melody took a deep breath of chocolate chips. "I bet your house smells delicious."

"Hank thinks so. I had to finally swat his hand so he wouldn't eat himself into an early grave. You know his little belly's already about to pop." She chuckled and started walking toward the festivities.

Melody could see the dunking booth midway down the field, and Applegate was pushing the red-dot trigger and watching the seat give way. It looked like he had everything under control. After all, how much preparation did it take to drop someone into a tank of water?

"You look pale. Are you feeling all right?"

"I'm fine, just rushing to get here is all."

They'd reached Esther Mae's booth. She set her crate down and plopped her fist on her purple pedal pushers. "I don't believe it for a minute. You are staying holed up out there at that old house way too much. I told Norma Sue and Adela just yesterday that I didn't like it one bit. A girl like you needs to be out playing some—mixing it up with a cute cowboy. You need dinner and a movie, slow walks by the creek. Hand-holding." She arched a brow. "That's how you find a man. Not hiding out in a house all by yourself, lost off in time, like you're doing. The future doesn't happen when you're living in the past."

Melody thumbed the plastic bag of cookies. "I'm fine, Esther Mae."

The redhead harrumphed. "Research is all well and good, but the past is the past. You're a young woman, and you need to be living life now. When's the last time you went out?"

"I've been out," she confessed, then realized she couldn't say anything.

"Not out as in a date."

It wasn't a question but a statement. Melody gave a small smile. She knew if she'd been out on a date the matchmakers would know it. "No. But, I've been having a good time." At least she'd tried to have a good time. "I'd better go help Applegate."

"Don't you let him put you up on that seat," she warned.

"You know what, Esther Mae, I might want to get on that seat."

"Oh, *really?*"

Melody glanced down the way. "Maybe."

Esther Mae laid a hand on her arm. "You know, Melody, we're family here in Mule Hollow. You bein' a quiet one like you are, well, me and the girls, we worry that you have things on your shoulders that weigh you down. You know you can talk to us. We're not just here to have a good time." She waved a hand when someone shouted out her name. "I mean, we're a little one-track when it comes to marrying off all our cowboys. But there is more to us than that."

Melody really didn't know what to say. This wasn't like Esther Mae. If anyone was going to offer a heartfelt back pat of encouragement it was Adela.

Esther Mae blushed. "I know what you're thinking. But, hon, there's always more to all of us than meets the eye. Sometimes you have to step out of your comfort zone and trust folks with your heart."

Melody felt dazed. "Thank you. I do have things on my mind. But—" She really wanted to open up, but she pulled back. This wasn't the place to spill her guts about issues so close to her heart. Especially since she'd already learned that sometimes doing that brought on more headaches than relief. Her thoughts filled with Seth. "I better go help App before he gets Stanley in that booth."

Esther Mae chuckled. "Now that, I'd pay to see."

Melody felt better as she strode through the crowd. The smells that only happen with a festival assaulted her senses and her stomach growled with the mixture of roasting peanuts, warming cotton candy sugar, grilling hot dogs. As she walked, more scents wafted her way and people called her name. She waved shyly, and her heart warmed despite all the turmoil that still waited to ambush her. Just being here among friends helped ease her emotions—maybe not for the long haul but there was comfort here. This was her town. And the people were good. She was glad she'd come.

## Chapter Seventeen

Seth drove up to the festival and took the last space across the street from Sam's. He didn't want to be here. He'd hardly slept, and his heart was heavy. God hadn't helped him come up with any easier answers. Like a coward, he'd let her walk away yesterday when he'd had something important to tell her.

He headed through the growing throng. He'd told App he'd help do whatever they needed him to do. Probably set up tables or something. "Hey, Stanley," he said as he passed the cotton candy booth. "How'd you get hooked up with that job?"

Stanley held up a stick of cotton candy that looked like it had tangled with a tree shredder. "I told them I'd do whatever it was they needed me to do. I should have known them was dangerous words."

"Same thing I told them." Seth hoped he wasn't going to be put in as sticky a situation as Stanley.

"You should go see Lacy. She's got the list."

"Thanks, but I think App has a job lined up for me."

Stanley hooted. "Oh, yeah, I got sugar on the brain. You're the other helper."

Seth suddenly had a revelation. He hadn't volunteered to be App's helper. He knew what that meant and he was smarter—at least he'd thought he was smarter than to get rooked into being the dunkee of the dunking machine! "Oh, no," he said. "I'm not getting in that bucket."

Stanley lifted a brow as he twirled a new paper cone around in the candy machine. "If you don't do it, then App's probably going to convince Melody to climb in thar."

"He wouldn't do that—would he?"

"App's got two choices. He can get a purdy girl up on that seat and have cowboys lined up to chuck balls and flirt with her. Or he can git a cowboy up thar and git purdy girls ta chunk balls at him and flirt. You know how App likes to get them quarters to pile up so he kin say he brought in the most money."

Seth glanced through the crowd. Down the way he could see App talking to Melody. She looked pretty in a yellow T-shirt and jeans. He wondered if she had any idea what App's plans were. "He is a devious little man."

Stanley chuckled. "Don't I know it. But it is fer a good cause. Every dime we raise goes to either the women's shelter or the fire department fer new equipment. Both of them's worthy causes, don't ya thank?"

Seth knew they were but spending all day getting dropped in a vat of cold water wasn't what he'd signed up for…on the other hand he wasn't about to let Melody take the fall, so to speak.

"You gonna do it?"

Seth pushed his hat back. "I'm not one to stand back and watch a lady get messed around."

Stanley reached out and walloped him on the shoulder. "Then what are ya waitin' on? Git over thar. With a good-lookin' fella like you and a beautiful girl like Melody workin' together on that booth, I bet the lines are gonna be longer than anywhar else in the whole festival."

Seth headed across the field. He was nervous about how he'd be greeted by Melody. He also wondered if she'd slept at all. Her dark hair shined in the sunlight, looking like a sheet of black silk when she moved her head to look up at App. The closer he got, the clearer it was that she looked pale. The strain was evident.

"Morning, App, Melody," he said, tipping his hat and searching her eyes for some sign that she was better. That her heart wasn't totally trampled down by the pain her brother had caused her. He hated seeing her hurting and holding her while she'd wept had broken his heart.

"Mornin', Seth. I wasn't so sure you'd show."

"Well, I just found out from Stanley what you have planned for me so maybe I should have gone back home."

Melody's eyes lit just a touch, and she bit her bottom lip.

App rubbed his thin chin and looked pleased with himself. "I figured if I had this breath of sunshine standin' here beside me, I'd have more leverage to get you up on that seat and I was right."

Seth smiled at the shocked expression on Melody's face.

"You ever been used as bait before?" He liked seeing the color flood back into her skin. Even if it was only temporary.

"Why would he use me as bait?"

She really didn't get it. That blew him away.

"I'm gonna go git me a cup of coffee. Y'all hold the fort down." App winked at Seth then strode into the growing crowd.

"So," he said, turning back to Melody. "How are you?"

"I'm making it."

"I hate that I upset you so badly yesterday."

She picked up a couple of balls out of the basket then dropped them back. "Apology accepted," she said, holding out her hand. "Truce?"

Seth's heart ached. He stared at her hand and wanted to take it more than almost anything—but he couldn't. "I didn't apologize."

Her posture went rigid, her chin lifted. "Then what did you mean?"

"Maybe now isn't the time to discuss this."

Her eyes flashed.

"Look," he said, very aware that the festival was about to start. "What you said has been bothering me. I should have said something yesterday, but you were just so upset that I couldn't do it."

"And that is?"

He cleared his throat and felt dread like he'd never felt before. But he knew no matter what he lost he had to be honest with Melody. "You said that you'd given up hope that God was going to help Ty." He had to force himself to go on. "You're right. I haven't walked in your shoes, but that may be exactly the way God wanted it when he crossed our paths. I can look at what you do from an objective point of view."

Her eyes narrowed. "And what would you see?"

"That you and your parents have done as God asks us all to do. You've given your heart and soul to helping Ty find his way. But now it's time to let him go."

"You said the same thing yesterday. You're right that this isn't the place to have this conversation."

"Melody. You have asked God for His help. Begged Him. Right?" He could tell she wanted to ignore him, but she didn't.

"Too many times to count anymore."

"And that's my point. You keep asking and praying for God to help your brother. But your brother hasn't done the asking. He hasn't even accepted that he's in the wrong. And if you keep doing what you're doing, he never will. Like you said, this will always be your life—dictated by Ty and his bad choices. You have to let him go and let him sink if that's what he wants to do. Even if it means he ends up on the street. You have to love him enough to let him go. And you have to trust God enough that you completely hand Ty over to Him and let Ty's life evolve."

"You don't—"

"Stop saying that," he snapped. He did know, he was living it right now and she didn't have a clue. "Your parents should have never left that burden on you. They should have put a stop to this a long time ago. Your brother is a jerk and needs to fall on his face—and you have to let him. Don't you get that? I'm telling you this because I care—" He ripped his hat off and rammed his hand through his hair. He'd lost it good, and this was the end.

"Seth!"

He glanced around and saw Susan weaving her way toward him. He looked back at Melody and wished they could be somewhere alone for this conversation. This hadn't been the time or the place for him to lose his temper. But it was done. Tearing his gaze away from the anger flaring in Melody's he looked back at Susan. "Hi."

"How are you today?" she said flipping her blond hair away from her face and smiling up at him. "You didn't tell me you were going to be here today. What a nice surprise."

"Um, yeah, looks like I'm going to be the target." He looked over at Melody, hating that he hadn't finished. "Have you ever met Melody Chandler?"

Susan held out her hand. "Hello, Susan Worth. I'm the vet around these parts. I come over from Ranger when Seth and the others need me. Isn't he a sweetie?"

That threw him, and he couldn't meet Melody's

accusing glare. The last thing she was thinking was that he was sweet.

"Oh, I hadn't noticed," she gritted out through clenched teeth.

"Oh, he is. He just likes to hide it behind that control-freak exterior," Susan said.

"Now *that* I noticed," Melody said, sarcastically.

Susan locked arms with his and squeezed. "So, how about you climbing up on that seat and letting me have a go at you?"

"Yes, Seth. Let's get this party started."

Seth looked from woman to woman. Fine. He wasn't sure what Susan was doing but he knew exactly what Melody was doing. The woman was so mad at him she'd *pay* people to come throw baseballs at his head if she could.

Melody watched Seth take his boots off then climb up into the dunking booth.

"Isn't he the cutest thing?" Susan said, then called out, "Now, don't fall in before I get loaded up here."

Seth grunted.

Melody hoped she dunked him on the first throw. And she hoped people kept dunking him all day long. Last night she'd been mad at God and Ty and everything in general. At this moment, she was furious with only Seth. The man had the gall to stand there and tell her if she'd have just let Ty go years ago then none of this would have happened. How dare he! How. Dare. He.

The minute Seth started climbing into the booth people stopped to watch. Several cowboys whooped it up.

"Hey, after me you fellas are gonna get in here."

Melody gave Susan the go-ahead. "He's all yours. Fire away."

Susan flirted with him, tossing the ball into the air and then she fired one in. It missed. Melody gritted her teeth, crossed her arms and watched as she threw four more balls. Seth bantered back and forth with Susan and several of the other women who moved close to the cage where they could get a close look at him. Three women actually asked him out during Susan's horrible display of athletic ability. Melody decided she was going to have to hit the red trigger button with her fist if Susan didn't get it on the next throw…goodness, the woman might be beautiful, full of life and apparently very available, but she couldn't hit the broad side of a barn.

And then finally the softball hit the target, and Seth dropped into the water like a rock. It was a beautiful sight.

\* \* \*

Two hours after he'd crawled into the dunking booth, Seth sloshed toward Melody instead of climbing back in. He'd watched as she'd enthusiastically recruited one woman after the other to step up and drop him in the tank. He knew she was upset with him. As a matter of fact, she was so mad at him, he was amazed to see that she'd come out of her shell in order to talk to everyone who passed by the basket of baseballs. Consequently she had a line of constant competitors. She hadn't spoken directly to him once since the balls had started flying. She cut her eyes at him many times. And he'd been glad to let her carry on to a point. But now, waterlogged and irritable, he decided it was time to stop the madness.

"I'm done," he said, picking up his boots and socks. He hadn't brought a change of clothes. He didn't even have a towel, and he was going to walk to his truck dripping wet. He wouldn't hear the end of this for ages from all his cowboy friends. He didn't wait for her to say anything as he walked off.

"Hey there, Seth," Norma Sue said as he passed her. "You've been a real trouper up there."

"Glad to do it," he grumbled and kept on going. He was going to go home, change clothes and head back out to the cave. He needed some time alone.

"I brought you a towel," Melody said, startling him as she jogged up beside him and held out a fluffy white towel.

"Where'd that come from?" He didn't slow down or take the towel.

"The ladies had them under the table for anyone who needed them."

Water dripped from his hair and his jeans weighed twenty pounds by themselves. "Thanks, but no thanks. I'll get my own towel when I get home. Don't you have someone else to drown back there?"

"Norma Sue took over."

Seth shot her a glare. She was having to stretch to keep up with him. He was being a jerk, but he wasn't really in the mood to fix it.

"Look," she said. "I'm mad, all right."

"Join the crowd."

She stopped walking and he heard her grunt. His truck was within sight, and he didn't slow down.

"Why are you doing this?" she asked, jogging to stand in front of him.

He stopped walking and looked up at the sky, asking for help. "If you haven't noticed, I care about you. When you care about someone, you want to protect them. I'm trying, but you won't let me. Why are you mad at me when you should be mad at your brother? He's the one ruining your life."

She didn't have a clue. She was staring at him like he was speaking a different language. He hung his head and tried to come to terms with the fact that Melody wasn't going to be a part of his life. How had he let himself get in so deep so fast?

"Have you ever stopped and thought that your brother's issues and your issues are separate issues? He needs to come to grips with his problems. That's painfully obvious. But, Melody, from where I sit, you're hiding issues of your own behind his. You're a Christian and yet you have no faith. Have you ever stopped to think that God might be waiting for you to get out of the way and trust on blind faith and have peace in your heart that He is in control?"

The defiance in her eyes ebbed, giving him hope that maybe she was at least listening. "You can't fix your brother. And I can't fix your problem no matter how much I want to…and it angers me. But truth is truth." He wanted to hold her, to kiss her. He wanted to tell her that hard as it was to believe, he'd fallen for her in the three short weeks they'd gotten to know each other. But he wouldn't. What use would it be? If she couldn't come to terms with her brother…there was no way he could ever let that lowlife dictate his life.

"I have to go." He strode to his truck and never looked back as he drove away.

## Chapter Eighteen

Melody didn't go back to the dunking booth after Seth left. Instead she went home—knowing Norma Sue had taken over meant the booth was in good hands. Better hands than her own.

She drove back to the stagecoach house, but she didn't go in. She walked to the back of the house and took the weathered stone stairs that had been laid so long ago down to the river. Walking to the edge of the water, she sank to the ground and prayed. Her thoughts were rushing through her mind with the speed of the water coursing past her, the feelings in her heart just as tumultuous. She'd been running—resorting to unplugging her phone…she was ashamed of herself. Had she resorted to being a coward? Was this what she'd become?

Seth had pointed out the obvious. She knew in

her heart he was right. She'd felt guilty that she'd been praying for her brother for years, but that her prayers were empty because she didn't believe God was going to answer them.

As a Christian, she was supposed to live by faith. Over and over through the Bible God repeated this truth. Christians had to live by faith.

*Truth was truth.* Seth's words came back clearly. Truth was, God had given her the command to trust Him in blind faith…

"Melody."

She turned to find Lacy standing midway down the steps. Her approach had been drowned out by the river noise. "Hey, what are you doing here?"

Lacy jogged down the last few steps and sank onto the rock beside her. "I was coming out of Sam's and heard the exchange between you and Seth. I started to mind my own business but God just kept thumping me on the head that I should come and see if there is anything I can do for you. I'm a pretty good listener, you know."

Melody's emotions swelled. She needed someone to talk to so badly. Lacy was so strong in her faith even when it had been tested. "I have a brother." Melody heard the words and felt relief in admitting them. Lacy placed a hand on her arm and squeezed gently.

"Tell me about him."

And she did. Melody told her everything. Everything she'd told Seth and everything she'd been feeling over the last few days. "I'm to the point that I feel so weak but angry at the same time. I'm twisted up inside most of the time. I've prayed and prayed for answers and for God to give me the strength to do what I need to do, but so far I still have nothing. What's worse now on top of everything is that I have these mixed-up feelings for Seth."

Lacy had listened so attentively and now she took a deep breath. "To think you've carried this all on your shoulders for so long. I could say, shame on you, because we're your family now and I wish you'd have let us all help—but I won't." She smiled kindly. "This was the path you had to take to get you to the point of truth. We each have to travel that path our own way, in our own time. As far as I know, there isn't any rushing that."

Melody let her words sink in. "Maybe you're right."

Lacy smiled. "Maybe. Listen, I don't have the answer here but I know God does. I know, though, that loving your brother, knowing he's ruining his life and not being able to help him has to be devastating for you. In your place, I don't know if I would have the strength to let him go, either…

even if it was in his best interest. But I can tell you this…God loves you, Melody. He hasn't forgotten you. He hasn't forsaken you and I think, listening to you talk, that that is what you think. Life happens. No matter how much we love someone, we can't make them make the choices we want them to make. We can only make the choices that are right for us. Romans 14:12 is one of the Bible verses that gives me comfort when things seem out of my control. It says, *'So then, each of us will give an account of himself to God.'* Short and direct, just the way I like things."

"But that can be interpreted that I shouldn't give up on helping Ty because if I do I'm accountable for it. And also at the same time it means Ty is accountable for his actions. I'm still running in circles with it." Melody took a deep breath and studied the water.

"Melody, dig deep and know that God has provided you with your answer. I know that He has. He has the answer. You'll know in your heart what is right for you. All this turmoil you're feeling is simply you fighting the truth as it pertains to you."

Melody looked away. What was the right choice for her? Not for Ty? And not for Seth?

"Have I helped you at all?" Lacy asked.

Melody leaned forward and hugged her. "More than I can express. I might not have my answers yet, but I feel better. I've felt like Seth is judging me about my life so far. He sees it in black and white, and there is no sympathy on his part for Ty. Talking to you I haven't felt that judgment."

"Good." Lacy hugged her tightly. "I guess I'll head on back to the festival. Being the girl heading up the committee, if there's a problem, things could get crazy if I'm not there."

This was so true. Lacy was indispensable in keeping things running smoothly. "Thanks for coming. I really needed someone to talk to."

Lacy stood up. "Any time. And this will work out. I have faith that God does have a plan. Call me if you need me again."

She turned to head up the steps then stopped. "You know, this is just a thought, but you said you were basically exhausted and feeling weak. Maybe that's where you need to be in order to see God's plan clearly. And maybe, just a thought, maybe someone to see things in black and white is the answer you need."

Seth couldn't let it go. All afternoon after having left Melody standing in the middle of the street at the festival, he'd worked like a dog clearing fence line, trying to work off his frustrations. He'd been hard on her. Yeah, truth was truth and he believed she needed someone pointing out to her the truth about her brother. But he'd been really angry when he'd spoken to her and that was wrong.

He hadn't walked in her shoes. He didn't know the heartache she was feeling, and so he shouldn't judge her. And that was what he'd done. He hadn't meant to but that didn't say it wasn't so. Period.

If he was man enough to dish it out, he was man enough to take it. When he finally worked through to this truth, the sun had disappeared and dusk was settling in. Soon they'd be shooting off fireworks at the festival. And in a perfect world he'd be sitting on his tailgate with Melody watching the display and then he'd kiss her and all would be well.

But this wasn't a perfect world. And he owed Melody an apology.

Thirty minutes later, after he'd cleaned up, he drove to Melody's. He told himself that no matter what was said he wasn't going to judge and he wasn't going to get angry. He was here to apologize and that was what he would do.

She opened the door before he'd made it up the steps. The warm light from inside the cabin bathed her in golden light and he had a deep yearning. How would it feel to have her welcome him home each night? He'd only spent three weeks in Melody's company and yet he knew she was the one for him.

Not that she'd ever feel that way about him.

He swept his hat off and worried it between his hands, working his fingers along the rim as he looked at her. "I've come to apologize," he said. "I was out of line today. Every day. Your brother is your business, and I had no right to impose myself into the situation."

"You want to come in?"

Her soft invitation was unexpected. "No. I just came to say that."

She nodded then surprised him by coming out onto the porch. She crossed her arms, walking barefoot to the edge of the porch. The porch light wasn't on, but the light from the windows stretched in oblong shapes across a portion of the porch and into the yard. She stayed out of the light.

"I've been reading my Bible all afternoon," she said, glancing at him before studying the night again. "Lacy came by and I talked to her. She saw us fighting and was worried. I told her about Ty."

"She's a good one to talk to."

She nodded, her arms tightening. "Do you know that I've had my phone off the hook since the other night?"

That startled him. "Why?"

She swung toward him. "Instead of facing Ty, I blocked him out. I didn't send him the money, and I didn't tell him I hadn't." She gave a harsh laugh. "I'm a regular ostrich. All these years I've been allowing myself to be a victim—I guess that's the right word. I don't know at this point, but I do know that I've been angry and put blame all over the place. But the reality is that I took the easy road. Supporting Ty's habit all these years was easier than watching him suffer."

She was in pain and it broke his heart. "Melody, you were doing the best that you could. I should never have been so hard on you."

"No. Actually, you were right. We all have to answer to God in the end, and no one can do it for us. I have to let Ty go. He was taught right from wrong and he's chosen over and over again this lifestyle…and why not? What's it costing him? Nothing. It's costing *me.* It cost my parents. But it's costing him nothing. Anyway, thank you for opening my eyes. I think you were actually an answer to my prayers—you were speaking hard truths that I needed verbalized."

What did he say to that? He wanted to be so much more to her than that, but the look in her eyes told him he didn't have a chance. The saying

"Don't shoot the messenger" probably wasn't going to help him here.

She started to go in and stopped. "I'm going home tomorrow."

"Home?"

"Yes. I'm going back to Katy to see Ty."

"What? But you just said?" What was he doing? Sticking his big mouth once more where it didn't belong.

"I'm going to tell him in person that I'm not giving him any more money or support. What I need to say to him can't be said over the phone."

"Let me come with you."

"This is something I have to do on my own."

"This is a bad idea."

"Why is that? Because it's not your idea?"

Seth's temper flared, and he had to check it. "He's your brother, but I don't know him. I don't trust him, and my gut tells me this is no good. If the guy is on drugs and you make him mad, you don't know how he's going to react. If he's been fooling with meth and coke and who knows what else, like I suspect, his brain isn't firing on all cylinders."

"I have to do this on my own. I have to be strong—isn't that what you've been telling me? I'm trusting God on this and I'm going. Alone."

Seth stepped toward her. Every fiber of his

being told him this wasn't a good idea. "Listen to me, Melody," the words came out gruff, as gravelly as all of the emotions grounding around inside of him. He took a chance and lifted his hands to cup her face. "You are important to me. I love you. I know we've only known each other for a short period of time but truth is truth. And that is mine." Her eyes widened, and she let out a small gasp. His heart was hammering, and he wanted to kiss her so bad he could hardly stand it. But now wasn't the time. There might never be a time. "I can't let you do this. Not on your own."

She pulled out of his arms. "You don't get a choice in this. Good night, Seth," she said then slipped inside and closed the door.

## Chapter Nineteen

As soon as Seth's taillights disappeared, Melody packed a suitcase and headed out of town. She wasn't taking the chance that he was going to be waiting on her porch bright and early the next morning. Call her foolish or whatever but she had to do this alone. She'd run from it long enough. And then, afterward, she could work through her feelings about Seth.

He'd said he loved her.

It was too unbelievable to believe.

And she was too mixed up emotionally to evaluate her emotions. Right now, she had so much of her past that she had to face. As she drove through the night, her thoughts circled backward to all the years she'd watched Ty work her parents. Looking back, she recognized his behaviors as the same. And yet she'd let him do the same with her.

She drove two hours to College Station before getting a room. She wasn't sure if she could sleep, but she knew she needed to try. After saying a prayer that Ty would be open to hearing what she had to say and that he would be ready to enter rehab, she sank into bed and fell asleep almost instantly. It had been an emotionally exhausting few days.

She was up by seven and dressed and in her car by eight. She pulled up in front of Ty's apartment in Katy a little after ten. It was sad. Her parents had left their home to Ty. They'd wanted to give him a place to live so that they wouldn't have to worry about him being homeless, but they'd borrowed so much money to send him to treatment that when they died the house had been taken to pay the debt. And now, it had come to this. Sitting in her car she felt calm. He had taken so much from them, and if they were still alive she knew he would still be taking. Yes, it could be said that it was the drugs but Melody knew that her brother had once clearly known what he was doing and he'd chosen to forsake everything dear for his own selfish purpose.

Why had it taken her so long to come to terms and to peace with what she had to do? She'd asked herself the question over and over again on the long drive. And Lacy's answer seemed the right one…she'd come to the reality of it when she was ready to accept it. And Seth had been the key to help her.

Again she didn't dwell on thoughts of Seth. This was about her and Ty. For the first time in years, she felt at peace. She hadn't made these choices for Ty. He had. And despite the fact his abuse had turned into addiction and some might argue that he couldn't make a responsible choice now that he was ruled by the drugs. Melody knew he knew the system better than anyone, knew how to ask for help and the steps involved in getting admitted into a program. He'd worked the system and everyone who'd ever loved him. He might not be ready to get off the merry-go-round but she was.

Her stomach hurt as she walked up the steps. Taking a deep breath, she knocked on the door. Her heart was pounding when he finally tugged it open. She almost gasped when she saw him. Hollow-eyed, drawn and dirty. Behind him the apartment didn't look any better.

"So you finally showed up," he sneered. "You bring my money? They're throwing me out tomorrow."

Anger and pity flooded her instantly. They were

so intermixed that she almost broke down. She swallowed hard. The prodigal son in the Bible had to learn a lesson on his own.

"I came to tell you in person that I love you, Ty. And because I love you I'm not paying your way anymore."

His eyes narrowed and his fist clenched. "You got all the money after Mom and Dad's wreck. You owe me."

"There wasn't any money. They'd mortgaged the house twice to pay for your rehabs and your addictions. And you didn't care." Her temper soared but she pulled back and held out a piece of paper. "Here are the numbers of several free drug programs. I've given them to you before on the phone, but I wanted to make sure you had them. This is the last time. You have to keep up with everything in your life now. I won't be taking calls from you anymore unless that call comes from inside a rehabilitation facility. If you'll agree, then I'll take you to one right now."

"Cut the drama. I'm not goin' to no rehab. They treat me like a dog, and they don't work anyway. You know it."

"They don't work because you won't let them. You have to want this and you know it. I can't do it for you."

"This is all Mom and Dad's fault—"

"This is *your* fault. All Mom and Dad ever did was love you. And you threw it all away."

He stepped toward her, his eyes wild, and Melody stepped back from the door realizing that maybe Seth had been right. Maybe she shouldn't have come here alone.

"Take this," she said, holding the list out and praying that she hadn't messed up. He snatched it and threw it on the ground.

"I'd rather be on the street than back in one of those places. And it'll be all your fault," he said.

"No, Ty. It won't be. All you have to do is ask for help and want it. The rehab will help you through the physical process and if you ask Him, God will be there beside you to give you strength." A calm came over Melody in that moment as if God had placed His hand on her shoulder reassuring her that she could let him go. She blinked back tears of sorrow for Ty, and in that moment she truly gave him to the Lord and put her hope in Him.

Her knees were weak as she turned and walked away.

"Odee," Ty called but she didn't look back. "C'mon, Odee, stop messing around and give me the check."

She got in her car, took a deep breath and then she drove away. His future was up to him now.

She had her own future to think about.

Seth was sitting on Melody's porch when she drove up at seven. Holding his temper in tight rein he pushed out of his chair. He was in his truck by the time she got out of her car.

He'd told himself this was her choice to go to her brother's alone. It was her business. He didn't have any business being mad, but it was like talking into the wind.

She looked tired and, despite his anger, he wanted to hold her so bad he almost broke. But she didn't want it. She'd told him as much by shutting him out.

"Seth," she said, coming up to his window.

He turned the ignition key. "You made it home."

"Yes. Have you been here long?"

He dipped his chin. "Long enough." How about twelve hours?

She looked at the ground. "I know you're mad at me and with good reason. I shouldn't have gone alone. You were right."

His heart jerked against his ribs like a bull against a gate. "You're all right, though? He didn't hurt you?"

She shook her head. "But I realized how easily he could have. If he'd have been really messed up, it could have gotten ugly. I'm sorry I didn't listen to you."

He held his tongue and stared straight ahead. He'd prayed fierce prayers that God would protect her. "I'm glad you're okay." He pulled the shifter into Drive but didn't let off the brake.

"Would you like to come in for coffee or something?"

"Nope. I've got cows to feed."

"Want some company?"

He nudged his hat off his forehead and fought off the urge to say "Yes, please!" "Not tonight. I'll see you around. I'm glad things turned out good for you."

"I know you're mad at me," she said.

"Nope. Not my business to be mad at you."

"Never stopped you before."

He heard the tease in her tone and wasn't pleased to hear it. "This isn't funny," he growled.

"You're right. It's not. And you're right I shouldn't have gone alone, and I've already apologized for that. But what is done is done, and for the first time in my life I feel peace about my brother. I can't help but feel good. Tomorrow he very likely will be without a home—which I hate. But I'm looking at it as the beginning of his awakening. He may have to sink as low as he can get before he surrenders to healing physically and spiritually. I'm praying somewhere in all of this he realizes that he needs the Lord in his life, too." She reached in through the window and placed her hand on his shoulder. "So, can you not be mad and just be glad that I've finally done what I needed to do? And what you wanted me to do?"

"I'm glad. I am. It's for the best. Get some rest. You look exhausted." She pulled her hand away, and he ignored the hurt he saw flash in those big violet eyes as he drove away. But they both needed some distance tonight. He'd realized something today, and it stung. He had no idea how she felt about him. She'd never really given him any confirmation that he was more than a treasure-hunting buddy to her…or some guy who bellyached about the way she chose to live her life. He'd told her he loved her, and she'd said nothing.

The phone was ringing when he walked in the door. "Yeah, it's about time you called," he snapped, having seen Wyatt's name on the display.

"You sound pleasant."

"You should see me in person."

His brother chuckled. "What's the matter, little brother?"

"You know exactly what's the matter."

"No, I don't. I moved a pretty lady in next door to you thinking she might be good for you and you sound like the world is coming apart at the seams. How can that be when Cole told me you were looking for a treasure?"

"We found a stinkin' cave and I could care less." Seth collapsed in his desk chair, knowing it was true. He only cared about one thing. Melody. "I love her."

"Excuse me. Did you say you loved her? Hey, she's only been out there—what, three weeks? I was hoping I could be making a match, but this is a little sudden, wouldn't you say?"

"I thought the same thing. But believe me, with everything that she and I have been through it feels like I've known her for at least three months."

"Three months seems quick to me. I was just hoping y'all got along and maybe in time something would work out. But three weeks?" He whistled, and Seth could see him slouching in his office chair.

"You don't sound very happy about it," Wyatt said after a moment of silence.

Seth told him about Ty, which got him another long whistle.

"No jokes, when you said y'all have been through a lot. So, she cut him loose."

"And she thinks everything is going to be great now."

"And you're not so sure?"

"Nope. For several reasons. Number one being that I have no clue if she has the same feelings for me that I have for her. Maybe I'm just the guy who happened to be here during all of this."

"I doubt that."

"What do you know?"

"Hey." Wyatt laughed. "I saw the potential the minute I looked into those Liz Taylor eyes."

"Yeah, I'll give you that."

"Would you relax? Who wouldn't love a grump like you? What else has you so tied up?"

"Same ole, same ole."

"You can't control everything, Seth."

"Yeah, I know."

"Well, maybe now would be a good time to relax and stop. What else?"

Seth laughed. "You make it sound so easy."

"Yep. Now what else? You've got to give me more than this. It sounds to me like things have been pretty heavy. And it has only been three weeks. What about this treasure? Cole filled me in on that interesting development."

"We've found the cave, but got sidetracked with everything else."

"Look, Seth, I know you. I'm startled by the fact you've come to these feelings so quickly. But you should just slow down."

Seth felt a headache building. "Wyatt."

"Yeah, you going to finally tell me what's really bothering you?"

Seth didn't say anything at first. He hated even admitting it. "Even if she ends up falling in love with me, I don't know if I can handle or want to handle her brother and his problems upending our lives."

"That is a problem. So you don't believe he's out of the picture like she told you?"

"I believe she's trying. That she's made great strides and is trusting the Lord to deal with it. But he's her brother. And even if by some miracle he finds his way and goes into rehab eventually…it'll give her the hope that he's healed. Until the next time he falls off the wagon or whatever it's called where drugs are concerned."

"When that happens, you deal with it. Why are you asking that? If you love her, you'll be there for her. You'll stand up and be the man she needs. You're the guy who has no tolerance where losers are concerned."

"This isn't about me. This is about what that continual strain does to her. You saw it. You just didn't realize what you were seeing. I didn't either until I started spending time with her. She was so torn up inside and beaten up emotionally. I don't know if I can watch that happen over and over again."

"Now I understand," Wyatt said, his exhaled breath heavy with regret. "That's—I'm not going to placate you, that's rough. And, Brother, that's not an answer I can help you with."

Seth took a deep breath. "I know. But at least you helped me face it. Until you called, I hadn't fully faced the concern. Look, I'll talk to you later."

"Hey, you take care, and I'll say a prayer for you…for both of you."

"Maybe you could say a prayer for her brother, too."

"Goin' up right now."

Seth clicked the disconnect and set the phone on his desk. And then he dropped to his knees and prayed his own prayer.

## Chapter Twenty

Seth was just finishing giving his men their orders for the day when Melody drove over the cattle guard. "We're going to have to stop meeting like this," he said, trying to be light as he moved to meet her. His heart had started doing loopy loops the instant he saw her.

"Hi, cowboy," she said, leaning against the fender. Her silver Mustang had seen better days, but with all the money she'd paid out to her brother all these years she probably hadn't had a new car on her list of things to buy. "You ready to load up?"

He lifted a brow and crossed his arms over his chest. It was either that or he was going to get in trouble for hauling her into his arms. "We going somewhere?"

"We've got a treasure to find, remember."

"Oh, I do seem to recall we had that on our agenda."

"Then let's load up and hit it. I've got sandwiches and water. And don't even think about continuing to be mad at me. I thought about it and today's a new day."

Her eyes were dancing, and he couldn't say no to her. "Then let's go. All the equipment is still in the back of my truck."

She reached in the car and pulled out her little insulated lunch box then sauntered past him. He watched her, stunned.

"Well, what are you waiting on?"

"Oh, nothing. Just glad you're here." And that was the truth. He had his worries, and the fact that she was acting so chipper had him a little worried that she was trying too hard not to think about what was going on in her brother's life today. But none of that discounted the fact that he was really glad she was here, smiling and teasing him.

"You know what?" he said, holding her door open as she slid into the seat.

"What?"

"I think Stanley might have a metal detector. I seem to recall him talking about taking it up as a hobby some years ago but haven't heard anything since. Let's swing through town and ask him."

"But that would mean him and App might be suspicious."

He twisted the ignition key and listened as the truck fired to life before looking at her. "I think that would be just fine."

Her eyes widened. "I don't believe you just said that."

"Yeah, me either, but today is a new day."

They didn't say anything for a couple of heartbeats, just looked at each other.

"Yes, it is," she said finally. "Let's go find a treasure."

He already had and he knew it. They were halfway to town before either of them spoke.

"Your grandmother was a strong woman."

He didn't have to ask which one she was talking about. "Yeah, she was. I've been thinking about her. How she wrote those journals documenting the history so carefully. So richly. She sounded like she enjoyed her life. Even though it must have been hard."

He nodded but didn't say anything, too curious as to where her thoughts were going.

"And yet she had this whole other thing going on at the same time. What happened to her? I never asked that?"

"She died of a fever. Grandpa Mason was about fifteen, I think."

"That would correlate to when the journals stopped being written. About 1888. I wonder if she hid the journal and the treasure map right before she died or if that was the hiding place for it all those years. You know, to keep prying eyes off of it." She smiled. "You get your desire for privacy from way back."

He hitched his brow. "Seems that way. But I've been wondering the same thing about the hidden journal. Honestly, and sadly, the stories passed down weren't about Jane. She was a good mother and a hard worker who obviously loved her family to strive so hard to keep them together. Despite the fact that she had a husband with a gambling problem. And a problem giving up on what proved to be a wild-goose chase for him."

Melody turned in her seat, and he glanced at her as town came into view on the horizon. Its brightly colored buildings stood out in the early morning sunlight. "So, Oakley, as far you know, died a few years later."

Seth had to come clean. "Yeah, he did and…he loved campfire stories and always told one about saddlebags of gold being buried on the land. The story has been passed down through the ages as his favorite."

Melody stared at him. "You knew this all along?"

He creased his forehead and nodded. "I didn't tell you because we didn't really believe the story. From what we've always believed, he was the king of tall tales and this was just one of those tales."

"What about his son Mason? He worked so hard beside your grandmother and obviously passed these stories down to his son…Oakley must have been loved by both your grandmother and Mason. There's nothing in either journal to dispute that. She doesn't say anything in them that is detrimental to him."

"He was a loser, but he must have been a heck of a guy," Seth said. "Wyatt takes after him, on the likable side. He's not a gambler although he tends to be great in the courtroom because of his ability to bluff his way out of most situations."

Melody chuckled. "I can see that about him. I liked him very much."

"The feeling was mutual."

She took a deep breath. "It was almost as if he looked at me and knew what I needed even before I did. I really needed to be out there."

Seth reached over and squeezed her shoulder. "He's like that."

"So," she said, plopping her hands on her thighs. "If Oakley was as likable as Wyatt, we both know why his son and his wife adored him despite his shortcomings. They both knew he had dreams of better days for them."

"You might be right about that. I guess we'll never know."

"That's what I hate about researching history, coming to a brick wall and not being able to continue the story."

Seth pulled up in front of Sam's. As usual, Applegate's and Stanley's trucks were sitting out front, and he could see them in the window of the diner bent over their checker game. "What about our story?" he said, reaching for her arm when she'd already opened her door.

"I—" she placed her hand over his "—I need time. My emotions are knotted up and—"

"It's okay. I get it." And he did. Everything had happened so fast and furious and he knew she had to be torn up inside despite the brave front she was putting on for him. "We'll move slow."

She nodded. "Thank you. I'd like that."

He touched her cheek, loving the feel of her skin against his fingertips. He cocked his head toward the diner. "Let's go stir up some help."

"Or trouble," Melody said, lightly.

Seth grinned. "I think that sounds like fun." And he did.

"Shor, I got a metal detector," Stanley said, pausing as he dipped a handful of sunflower seeds from the five-pound bag sitting on the edge of the table.

"You got a treasure?" Applegate turned his hearing aid up as Stanley and Sam stared at Melody and Seth.

Melody wasn't certain how to answer the question. Sure, it had been Seth's idea to come ask if Stanley owned a metal detector but did he really want to expose the possibility of a treasure on his land? He'd been so against it before. She glanced at him, letting him give whatever answer he wanted.

"Yes, I do," he said, draping his arm around her waist and tugging her close. His eyes captured hers and sent her heart thudding. He was talking about her, and everyone knew it. He'd said he loved her. Her, unremarkable as she was, it was so hard to believe. Not only had it been such a short time but because she was not the type of woman she'd envisioned him with. She was not the Susan Worth-type…beautiful, playful, remarkable…and yet she wasn't so sure about that anymore. She felt differently since meeting Seth. Since coming to terms with her life, with Ty. With letting go. She felt renewed—and that was remarkable.

Maybe remarkable was a state of mind.

"How would you fellas like to see a cave?" he asked.

"You ain't josh'n us?" Sam asked, slapping a dishrag over his shoulder.

"Nope. Me and Melody found a cave. And we found it because she discovered a treasure map hidden in the stagecoach house."

Stanley and App stood up so fast they sent sun-flower seeds and checkers flying.

"Well, what are ya waitin' on?" App called, shooing them toward the door. "You don't ask a question like that to a herd of bored ole codgers like us and then dawdle."

Melody jumped out of their way, right into Seth's arms as he backed out of the stampede toward the door. She stared up at him and he grinned. "What'd I tell you about the crazies and loonies coming at the mere mention of a treasure?"

Melody's heart warmed with affection. "Oh, but they're such adorable loonies," she said, looking up at Seth and feeling so happy, so right.

Outside Sam could be heard excitedly telling

some hungry would-be patron that the diner was closed for business. He had a treasure hunt to tend to.

"I think that's our cue," Seth said. "Are you with me?"

She nodded. "Oh, yes, I'm definitely with you."

"Don't touch anything," Norma Sue said, barking orders to the small troupe of eager treasure hunters they'd picked up as they walked out of the diner. Norma Sue and Esther Mae had been coming in for coffee when they were all climbing into Seth's and Applegate's trucks. Not to be left behind, the two ladies had immediately hopped into the backseat of Seth's Dodge.

They'd stopped at Stanley's, where he'd proudly shown them his top-of-the-line, something-or-other gold-standard metal detector. Melody couldn't remember the name brand that he spouted off but it must have really meant something to folks in the know. All she could say was he was really adorable showing it off, and she really hoped it was as good as it was supposed to be.

Seth had parked as close as he could get to the cave, and then he'd led the way down the ravine toward the cave. And now here they were.

"We ain't touchin' nothin'," App said, shining his flashlight about the interior room.

Sam held the lantern high, and everyone gasped over the whole golden light effect. Melody felt oddly disconnected. She'd been so thrilled about the entire idea of the treasure hunt when she'd first found the map, but nothing had unfolded the way she'd expected a treasure hunt to unfold. She wasn't the person she'd been when she'd started this journey.

"Turn that thing on," Esther Mae said, eyeing the metal detector.

"Stand back," Stanley warned, puffing his chest out as he flipped the switch. "If thar's treasure buried in here, this baby'll find it."

"Even if we don't find a treasure this has been some kind of fun," Norma Sue said. "You know I can't believe y'all had all this goin' on, and we didn't know anything about it."

Applegate grunted. "Y'all was on yor boat trip."

"So I guess you're going to tell me and Esther Mae that you boys knew about this?"

Sam looked at her. "We didn't know about *this*." He indicated the cave. "But we knew something more important was goin' on."

Melody smiled at Seth and he winked. "They knew the day after you told me you weren't leaving the property that I was caught, hook, line and sinker."

"Yep. We knew it, all right," Stanley called over his shoulder as he moved about the room.

Melody wrapped her arms around Seth's waist and hugged him. She wanted to kiss him so much. To tell him she loved him but not with a room full of people. And not before she had time to talk to him about something that she knew she had to say.

"Can I talk to you outside?" she asked.

"You kids have fun," Seth said, taking her hand and leading her out through the exit into the outer room and into the sunlight.

"I didn't mean to embarrass you back there," he said the minute they were out of earshot. "I know this has all been a little fast and I plan to slow everything down after today."

"Seth, I love you, too," Melody blurted out and then felt her cheeks warm. "Did you mean it when you said you loved me?"

"With all my heart!" He proved it by swooping her into his arms and kissing her.

Melody melted as his lips touched hers. Her world spun as she answered his kiss with her own, and she knew this was the treasure she'd been looking for all of her life. But she pulled away and steadied her nerve. "I have to ask you something," she managed as her heart raced with love and yearning so strong she felt like she'd fallen into the river and was racing downstream.

"Anything," he said, his voice husky.

"I don't know what you're thinking, but before I let this go any further we need to talk about Ty."

He exhaled and leaned his head against hers. "I think so, too."

Her heart sank at the sound in his voice. "I'm not the person I was when I first came out here. I'm stronger. I know what I want out of life, and I know what I don't want. I'm not going to ever let Ty's problems run my life again. And I don't really want to have conversations about him. But, like we keep saying, truth is truth and he's my brother. And I can never promise that I will completely eradicate him from my life. Could you live with that? I mean, would you be willing to continue our relationship—see where it goes—knowing that?"

She held her breath as she watched his eyes soften with love. It was unmistakable.

He kissed her cheek. "I can't lie and tell you I didn't think about that. I won't stand back and let him treat you like he treated you before. I'll always be here as a barrier. But it was not knowing if I could handle watching him tear at you emotionally that was the problem."

"I'm going to be okay if you're there beside me."

He placed his hands on either side of her face and smoothed her hair back. "I really think you are. You're so much stronger than you thought you were."

"Thanks to you."

"And thanks to you I think I have a little more compassion than I did have. But here's the deal—when you marry me."

She laughed, she couldn't help it. "A little bold, aren't you?"

He smiled. "I'm just staking my claim. You're one treasure I don't plan to lose, baby."

"Oh, Seth." She stood on her tiptoes and hugged him tightly.

"But listen to me," he said against her ear, hugging her. "You will always be my priority from this day forward." Holding her shoulders, he stood her away from him and looked into her eyes. "That means I'm serious when I say I won't stand for anyone hurting you—no one. Can you handle that?"

For the first time in her life, tears of happiness filled her eyes. "Oh, yes, I can handle that," she said. "I love you so much."

"That's all the treasure I'm interested in," he said.

And then Seth, the love of her life, kissed Melody like she was the most remarkable woman God had ever created.

# Epilogue

The call came four weeks later on the day Melody was preparing for her wedding. It was from a facility on the coast of Texas and the caseworker was calling to tell Melody that her brother had entered the program. He hadn't asked to call her himself but had simply wanted the caseworker to let Melody know that he was there and that this time it was because he wanted to be. Melody cried silent tears and hope flickered in her heart.

She'd spent the happiest days of her life over the last month as she and Seth had prepared for their wedding day. She thought of Ty, but she'd successfully detached herself emotionally from dwelling on wondering about what was happening in his life. Instead she'd continued to pray for him, believing that good could come to him if he'd just seek it.

After thanking the caseworker for calling, she hung up the phone and said a prayer for her brother. She asked for God to strengthen him and put people around him in the center who could help him. He had a long way to go, but for the first time in his life, her brother had made the right choice. On his own.

And so had she. By the end of the day, she would be Mrs. Seth Turner. She closed the journal she'd been reading when the phone rang and gently ran her hand over the weathered leather. They hadn't found any gold inside the cave. But they'd found evidence that once there had been some. It was one of those legends that would forever go unsolved, but as for her and Seth they felt eternally grateful for what they'd found in the search.

"Melody, are you in here?" Lacy called from the front door.

"I'm in here."

"Well, hop to it, girlfriend. We have a wedding to get you to—" Lacy stopped in the doorway. "You look beautiful!"

Melody stood up and looked down at her wedding dress. "I couldn't help myself. I knew I was supposed to get dressed at the church, but I wanted to put my dress on here."

"It's your day. You can put your dress on anywhere you want to."

Melody smiled, grabbed her veil and let Lacy hustle her out of the stagecoach house and into her pink Cadillac.

"You don't mind if the top is down?" Lacy asked, helping Melody get into the front seat without getting her dress dirty. "I just thought it's such a beautiful day, and you know me— there's nothing that makes a special day more special than a ride in the sunshine. Kind of puts you close to God," she said, jogging around the front of the car.

Melody watched as her friend hopped over the driver's door and landed with a plop in the seat. "I think you're absolutely right. Today is the perfect day for a ride. I feel so thankful for what God has done for me."

"Then tighten up your belt, and let's hit the road," Lacy said and punched the gas pedal. Instantly, the big tank of a car shot down the road like a pink rocket.

Melody laughed into the wind. Seth was waiting at the church for her at the end of the road. She felt like she was soaring as she held her veil in the air and let the wind stream through it. She was flying along a road that was over two hundred years old. So many people had traveled down it on their way across Texas in search of their futures. Just like she was doing—except Melody had found hers and it was with Seth.

As she felt the sun on her face and the wind in her hair, she knew that of those who'd ever traveled this road, she was the happiest of all.

It was remarkable. Wonderfully, happily remarkable.

\* \* \* \* \*

Dear Readers,

Thank you so much for spending time with me and the gang here in Mule Hollow! As you know, I love to keep you guessing about where my next stories are going to take you, and this story is taking you where I really didn't want to go. But I always write from my heart and Melody's story in many ways could be my own story or that of thousands of others across the country whose lives have been touched by the drug abuse of someone we love.

Melody was on the brink of breaking from the strain of dealing with her brother's addictions, and yet she knew that she had to make a change in her life. As a Christian she was especially torn about how she should handle her situation. Seth came along and gave her the strength to trust God even when it felt uncomfortable for her to make the hard choices.

I pray that if you are making hard choices in your life, God will give you a peace about it and guide you. And that you will have the strength to give your heartache to Him. And I pray with hope in my heart for you as you do so.

I love hearing from readers, and though I always fear I may not get to reply to everyone, I try. But please know your letters mean the world to me and touch me as I hope my books are touching you. You can reach me at P.O. Box 1125, Madisonville, Texas 77864, at www.debraclopton.com or through the Steeple Hill address.

Until we meet again, may God give you hope and peace,

*Debra Clopton*

## QUESTIONS FOR DISCUSSION

1. Melody loves history. Why?

2. Seth believes in his privacy. He believes that although he owns a piece of history, he shouldn't have to alert the world. What do you think?

3. Seth can't believe he's not noticed Melody before now. Have you ever known someone from a distance, and when you finally get to know them wished you'd made the effort sooner?

4. Melody doesn't understand why God hasn't answered her and her parents' prayers for her brother. Have you ever had prayers that desperately needed answering, and had to wait until God's timing was right to see His answer? Are you still waiting to see His answer?

5. In such a situation as Melody's—in which her brother seems to have neither remorse nor the desire to help himself and yet feels entitled to hold her life captive—how do you think, as a Christian, she handled herself?

6. Melody feels hopeless, trapped, victimized and angry. Can you see why she is angry?

7. Melody's parents let Ty's problem dictate their lives, and in doing so they put Melody's life on the back burner, so to speak. What do you think about this? How do you think parents in this situation should handle such a problem?

8. If you are a parent of someone addicted to drugs or alcohol or you are a sibling to a brother or sister with addictions, how do you feel? Especially when others try to offer advice that makes you feel judged?

9. Despite her anger, Melody is still letting Ty's addictions—his life choices—run and ruin her life. When Seth tells Melody she has to let Ty go, he is looking at what it is doing to Melody. At some point in a situation like this a person has to stop enabling the addict. Do you agree? Seth knows he loves Melody and that telling her this could harm the relationship they've begun. Yet he knows because he loves her that he must tell her or he will be doing her a disservice. What do you think?

10. How does Melody react to Seth's strong position on this?

11. Seth doesn't think he can deal with the ongoing challenges he knows Melody will face for the rest of her life when it comes to Ty. When addiction creeps into a family, it sadly is almost never completely eradicated. Seth understands the toll the ups and downs will take on her— that she will probably always suffer pain because of her brother's choices. But then he realizes that he wants to be there for her in the good times and the bad times. I loved that about him. What do you think?

12. If you've ever had to let someone you loved go, was there a verse in the Bible that helped you deal with the decision? Do you have anything good to share about the experience? Or are you still struggling with the decision? If so, ask for prayer and to be lifted up as you continue to remain strong while letting God have control.

13. As a Christian group, can you see some way that you can be of help to your sisters and brothers who are suffering with this issue?

What types of support for the families can we as a church offer?

14. The hard parts of this story aside, I enjoyed the history of the lost loot in this story. It is interesting to me that so much treasure could actually be reported as still being out there, buried beneath our feet! Do you enjoy treasure hunting? Do you know anyone who does? Personally, I've toyed with going on the hunt myself...but I have too many books to write and too little time, so I'll have to leave the treasure hunting up to you. If you've had an interesting find, please write and tell me about it. I would love to hear about your adventure!

Dumped via certified letter days before her wedding, Haley Scott sees her dreams of happily ever after crushed. But could it turn out to be the best thing that's ever happened to her?

*Turn the page for a sneak preview of*
*AN UNEXPECTED MATCH*
*by Dana Corbit,*
*Book 1 in the new*
WEDDING BELLS BLESSINGS *trilogy,*
*available beginning August 2009*
*from Love Inspired®.*

"Is there a Haley Scott here?"

Haley glanced through the storm door at the package carrier before opening the latch and letting in some of the frigid March wind.

"That's me, but not for long."

The blank stare the man gave her as he stood on the porch of her mother's new house only made Haley smile. In fifty-one hours and twenty-nine minutes, her name would be changing. Her life as well, but she couldn't allow herself to think about that now.

She wouldn't attribute her sudden shiver to anything but the cold, either. Not with a bridal fitting to endure, embossed napkins to pick up and a caterer to call. Too many details, too little time and certainly no time for her to entertain her silly cold feet.

"Then this is for you."

Practiced at this procedure after two days back

in her Markston, Indiana, hometown, Haley reached out both arms to accept a bridal gift, but the carrier turned and deposited an overnight letter package in just one of her hands. Haley stared down at the Michigan return address of her fiancé, Tom Jeffries.

"Strange way to send a wedding present," she murmured.

The man grunted and shoved an electronic signature device at her, waiting until she scrawled her name.

As soon as she closed the door, Haley returned to the living room and yanked the tab on the paperboard. From it, she withdrew a single sheet of folded notebook paper.

Something inside her suggested that she should sit down to read it, so she lowered herself into a floral side chair. Hesitating, she glanced at the far wall where wedding gifts in pastel-colored paper were stacked, then she unfolded the note. Her stomach tightened as she read each handwritten word.

"*Best?* He signed it *best?*" Her voice cracked as the paper fluttered to the floor. She was sure she should be sobbing or collapsing in a heap, but she felt only numb as she stared down at the offending piece of paper.

The letter that had changed everything.

"Best what?" Trina Scott asked as she padded into the room with fuzzy striped socks on her feet. "Sweetie?"

Haley lifted her gaze to meet her mother's and could see concern etched between her carefully tweezed brows.

"What's the matter?" Trina shot a glance toward the foyer, her chin-length brown hair swinging past her ear as she did it. "Did I just hear someone at the door?"

Haley tilted her head to indicate the sheet of paper on the floor. "It's from Tom. He called off the wedding."

"What? Why?" Trina began, but then brushed her hand through the air twice as if to erase the question. "That's not the most important thing right now, is it?"

Haley stared at her mother. A little pity wouldn't have been out of place here. Instead of offering any, Trina snapped up the letter and began to read. When she finished, she sat on the cream-colored sofa opposite Haley's chair.

"I don't approve of his methods." She shook the letter to emphasize her point. "And I always thought the boy didn't have enough good sense to come out of the rain, but I have to agree with him on this one. You two aren't right for each other."

Haley couldn't believe her ears. Okay, Tom wouldn't have been the partner Trina Scott would have chosen for her youngest daughter if Trina's grand matchmaking scheme hadn't gone belly-up. Still, Haley hadn't realized how strongly her mother disapproved of her choice.

"No sense being upset about my opinion now," Trina told her. "I kept praying that you'd make the right decision, but I guess Tom made it for you. Now we have to get busy. There are a lot of calls to make. I'll call Amy." Trina dug the cell phone from her purse and hit one of the speed dial numbers.

Haley winced. In any situation, it shouldn't have surprised her that her mother's first reaction was to phone her best friend, but Trina had more than knee-jerk reasons to make this call. Not only had Amy Warren been asked to join them downtown this afternoon for Haley's final bridal fitting, but she also was scheduled to make the wedding cake at her bakery, Amy's Elite Treats.

Haley asked herself again why she'd agreed to plan the wedding in her hometown. Now her humiliation would double as she shared it with family friends. One in particular.

"May I speak to Amy?" Trina began as someone answered the line. "Oh, Matthew, is that you?" *That's the one.* Haley squeezed her eyes shut.

\* \* \* \* \*

*Will her former crush be the one*
*to mend Haley's broken heart?*
*Find out in AN UNEXPECTED MATCH,*
*available in August 2009*
*only from Love Inspired®.*

*Love Inspired*

# SUSPENSE

RIVETING INSPIRATIONAL ROMANCE

These contemporary tales
of intrigue and romance
feature Christian characters
facing challenges to their faith...
and their lives!

**Four new Love Inspired Suspense titles are
available every month wherever books are
sold, including most bookstores, supermarkets,
drug stores and discount stores.**

Steeple
Hill®

Visit:
**www.steeplehillbooks.com**